MAKING A KILLER

ACID VANILLA FLASHBACK 1

MATTHEW HATTERSLEY

BOOM BOOM PRESS

For AJH x

A NOTE ON MAKING A KILLER

Thank you for downloading this book.

Whilst this novel is complete and can stand alone, it is the prequel to the first book in the Acid Vanilla series: *The Watcher*

If you haven't yet read *The Watcher* I do urge you to do so before you read *Making a Killer*. You'll find this book makes more sense and you'll appreciate the references much more if you do.

You can get a copy HERE

Thanks, Matthew

I

The young girl froze, at once blinded by confusion and rage. White light danced at the corner of her vision. White heat shot through her veins and up her spine.

Was this really happening?

How was this real?

As the room swam back into focus, she saw the woman lying, twisted and broken on the kitchen floor. Her mother. From this angle, the girl couldn't tell whether she was unconscious or dead.

As her awareness spread, she saw a dark figure standing over her mother, saw the pools of blood, the spatter marks up the wall and across the floor. Gasping herself into full alertness the girl's eyes flittered around the scene, already fully open to the cruelty of the world.

The man heard her whimper and turned around. He was tall but slim, wearing a white vest and navy pinstripe trousers that hung open at the crotch. He looked the girl up and down and a vile, leering smile spread across his wet chops.

"Hello there. Round two, is it?"

The girl stiffened as a surge of chaotic energy shot up her spine and into her chest. The noises in her head were suddenly cacophonous. A million chattering voices telling her to act, to strike, to run. Always the same at times of such stress.

As the man stepped across her mum's fallen body, the girl saw he held a wine bottle in his hand. It was covered in blood. Her mum's blood.

The red mist took hold as he lunged towards her, but she was able to evade his clutches. She had a small frame, but she was strong, athletic, and was now buoyed by a primeval rage that scared and excited her in equal measures. She glanced down at her mum's body, at the dotted bruises on her bare thighs and the tops of her arms. Finger marks, where the bastard had held her down. Where countless men had done the same.

With a grunt, the ogre came at her again, but she twisted away leaving him to stumble into the breakfast bar where he dropped the wine bottle.

His first mistake.

The bottle rolled across the blood-soaked tiles and came to a halt by the girl's foot. In one movement she scooped it up and flipped it over, holding it tight by the neck.

This had to stop. She had to stop it.

"Don't do anything stupid," the man growled. "Give me the bottle."

The girl smashed the bottle off the corner of the breakfast bar like she'd seen people do in the movies. Sharp shards of glass splintered into the room. A fragment flew up and hit her, slicing the skin on the upper part of her jaw, next to her ear. She didn't feel a thing. Plus, the bottle was lighter now easier to control, and with sharp jagged edges jutting out where the base had been. A deadly weapon in the wrong hands.

In the right hands too.

The man edged towards her. Ready to pounce. Whatever happened next, it had to happen fast. She looked up through her hair as the vile *beast loomed down on her. His hands were open. Thick fingers flexing for control. He wanted the bottle. He wanted to stop her. Just like he'd stopped her poor mother, bleeding out on the floor. The girl glanced at the ceiling, told herself, stay strong. Then, with a banshee scream, she launched herself at the man.*

The long corridor was cold and dark and there was nothing on the walls except old, yellowing paint. To further highlight the morose atmosphere a strong stench of bleach stung the girl's sinuses along with deeper, more heady smells of soiled clothes and body odour. It was the exact sort of décor, and the exact atmosphere, the young girl had expected. That was one thing, she thought, as she was led to a door at the far end of the corridor by the brusque guard - she was, in some ways, prepared for this hell.

But she was tired. So tired. The journey from London had been a long one and she'd been on high alert the entire time, what with her being the only passenger on the minibus and the sleazy driver staring at her at every opportunity. He did little to hide it either. Little piggy eyes in the rear-view mirror. Staring at her legs. Her breasts. She'd wanted to say something. Had felt compelled to. But she'd resisted. Pick your battles, that's what her mum had told her. And there was little point in making things worse for herself.

They got to the end of the corridor. Through the frosted glass of the door the girl could make out a figure - moving around as if lifting things from a bookcase. The guard grabbed the girl by the shoulders. Her sharp nails dug into the taught flesh on her collar bone.

"Here we are," the guard said, stiffening. She reached up and knocked on the glass. "I'll wait for you outside. This won't take long. The Governor has a meeting today. So, you'll meet with her tomorrow."

The girl nodded. She'd heard about the Governor, who all the girls in the remand centre referred to her as Jabba, though no one had explained to her where the name arose from. She'd heard the woman was small and wiry. Nothing like that grotesque slug from the Star Wars films.

"For Christ's sake, what the hell is she playing at?" the guard reached up and rapped her bony knuckles on the glass. Harder this time. She whispered under her breath, "Dithering idiot."

The girl looked at the floor. Once more she considered saying something in response but decided against it. She was here. There was no changing that. Best to keep her head down and her mouth shut. Have her time here go by as quickly as possible. Without too much upset. That was her hope. And her promise.

The figure moved towards the door and opened it, revealing a short, slight woman with a kind face.

"Oh, hello' she chimed, in a voice that matched her demeanour. "Were you waiting?" Her hair was scraped up into a tight bun which made her look old, and from a different era. She wore a starched white blouse and navy trousers, indicating she was some sort of nurse or medical person.

The guard nodded at the girl, keeping a tight grip on her. "The new arrival," she sniffed. "I've done her paperwork."

The nurse smiled at the girl. Albeit briefly. A friendly face at last. Though looks were deceiving. "Come in then, quickly. Close the door."

The girl followed her into the room and turned to get the door. The guard had pulled out some tobacco and rolling papers from her uniform and sat on a chair opposite. She glanced up at the girl but didn't react as she shut the door.

"Sit down," the nurse said. She didn't look up.

The girl did as she was told, taking a seat in front of a large wooden desk in the middle of the room. To her left, down the far side of the room stood a metal bed on wheels. The sort doctors use for examining patients. A blue curtain hung from the ceiling on an L-shaped rail and beyond this was a window so thick in grime and bird shit it provided scant light to the room. The girl kept her eyes on the nurse as she rooted through a large metal filing cabinet on the opposite side of the room. She pulled out a brown cardboard file and narrowed her eyes at the name.

"Alice Vandella? Is that you?"

The girl, Alice, nodded. "Yes." Her voice was croaky. She hadn't had a drink in over six hours. Hadn't spoken in over twelve.

The nurse walked over, reading the file notes. An expression of puzzlement twisted her face as she got to the end. Alice knew the look. The nurse was trying to marry the image of the young girl in front of her with the vicious beast she was reading about. She sat behind the desk, opposite Alice.

"I'm Nurse Kelly," she said, still scanning the notes. "You'll not see much of me after today. Unless you're hurt or ill for whatever reason. You know why you're here of course." She looked up. "Oh yes. How odd. Your eyes."

Alice didn't have a response. They'd been like this her whole life. She was used to the comments.

"I believe Vicky has already processed you," Nurse Kelly continued. "So, my job today is to give you a physical examination and answer any concerns or questions you might have. You'll be seen more regularly of course by our resident therapist. Once a week at first. Same time each week. Usually, an hour or so. Any questions?" Alice shook her head. "Good. Then I need you to go over to the curtain and get undressed. Underwear too. Here," she offered Alice a clear bag. "Put your stuff in there. You'll be able to change into regulation clothing once we're done."

Alice took the bag and shuffled over to the bed. She tried to draw the curtain, but it snagged halfway along the rail and wouldn't budge.

"Don't worry," Nurse Kelly told her. "Privacy isn't something you should be getting used to here."

Alice took a deep breath and got on with it. That was her plan. Acceptance. The key to survival.

After her arrest she'd railed against the world for weeks, months. Protested the unfairness of her predicament with whoever would listen. But no one was listening. That was the problem. The system looked at the crime, not the cause. So, she'd been sent here - a secure unit for criminally dangerous young girls.

When the judge passed sentence Alice had screamed the place down. She wasn't crazy, she told him. But trying to get the point across through tears and wails and gnashing teeth wasn't the best idea in the world. So, she'd made the decision. She'd accept her situation and do her time. Prove to everyone she wasn't crazy. She wasn't a threat. Six years and she'd be out. Back with her mum. Living a normal life. She ignored the fire raging in her belly. Told herself, it was normal for every cell in her body to tingle with feverish energy.

She got undressed and stuffed her clothes in the bag like she'd been told. Then she lay down on the bed. There were no sheets. The thin mattress was covered in a cold plastic veneer that stuck to her skin.

"Are you ready?" Nurse Kelly asked, walking over regardless and snapping a gossamer rubber glove over her wrist.

"Yeah, ready," Alice told her. And part of her was.

ONE

THE PHYSICAL EXAMINATION WAS BRIEF BUT INTRUSIVE AND
Alice gritted her teeth throughout, although nothing
untoward was found. After that Nurse Kelly asked her some
questions which she answered honestly. She wasn't a virgin;
had been with two boys on two separate occasions (brief but
intrusive). She'd never been pregnant, didn't smoke, or
drink, or do drugs.

She watched as Nurse Kelly wrote it all down on a
clipboard. She hadn't told her to get dressed yet. "What
about your moods?" the nurse asked, still writing. "Do you
ever feel angry for no reason?"

Alice thought about it. "Maybe. Sometimes." She
watched Kelly like a hawk. But she couldn't read her.

The next question hit her in the guts. "Do you ever think
about killing yourself?"

"Not really," Alice said. Then, more definite, "No."

Nurse Kelly looked at her through her eyelashes. Her
face was cold. "What about other people? Before the

Twelfth of May Nineteen-Ninety-Eight did you have any desire or drive to kill anyone?"

Alice shook her head. A little too emphatically perhaps, but she meant it. "No. I never. And then I was only trying to protect myself. Protect my mum."

Nurse Kelly put the clipboard down and made a disapproving noise. Like she didn't believe her. "Well, that's it from me. Vicky will now take you to your room. As I say if you keep your nose clean and stay healthy you won't see much from me. I suggest strongly you do both."

Alice nodded. "Can I get dressed now?"

"Yes of course. Here you go." She handed Alice a pile of clothes. Grey jogging bottoms and a grey sweatshirt. Plus, pumps, a white t-shirt, plain white knickers, and an elasticated sports bra. "They're your size," Nurse Kelly said. "Just about."

Alice slid off the bed and got dressed. The clothes smelt musty. Like they'd been washed but not dried properly.

"You know, you're a pretty girl, Alice," Nurse Kelly said, watching her get dressed. "Those eyes. What are you, Italian?"

"Sort of. My mum's dad." She stepped into the jogging bottoms and slipped on the regulation pumps. No laces. Too dangerous.

"Only fifteen." Kelly frowned. "You're one of the youngest girls we've got here Alice. That's going to mean something to the others. If you want my advice, sign up for as many jobs as you can get. Keep busy. Keep out the way."

Alice pulled the sweater over her head. It swamped her but she gave Nurse Kelly her best smile. "Thanks."

"Righto, well you run along now." The nurse opened the

door and looked across the hall, speaking to the guard. "No issues here."

The guard, Vicky, stood up as Alice got to the doorway. "Fine," she said. "Come with me girl."

Alice followed the guard down a labyrinth of long, stark corridors before the space opened out into a large hall. There were small windows along one side that looked out into the grey sky. Nothing else. On the opposite wall, two vending machines offered a depressingly meagre selection of snacks. It reminded Alice of the dining room at school. Same beige vinyl floor. Same strip lights. Placed at intervals along the cardboard tiled ceiling. There were maybe forty tables in rows, with an orange plastic chair on either side.

"This is the visiting room," the guard said. "Your visiting time will be Tuesday morning. One hour. Any kin you have will have been informed the same."

Alice hoped her mum would be able to visit soon. Though how she'd get here was uncertain. She had been doing better recently. Was out of the hospital. Able to walk. But Alice still worried. Something had changed in her. Having your only daughter locked up might have done it.

They moved through the room and Alice waited at the far side as the guard removed a large bunch of keys from her belt and unlocked the door. Then they were down another long corridor. The smell of bleach once more. Stronger now. They walked past a large set of double doors.

"Here's where you'll eat your meals," Alice was told. "Breakfast, lunch, dinner. You can also congregate there between ten and twelve, and two and nine. There's a television set. Games. If you like that sort of thing. After nine all girls are in their rooms."

They continued further down the corridor and through another locked door. This time it opened out onto a long room with doors along each side.

"This is your block," the guard said, turning to look at Alice. "Block C. You've been put in with a girl called Karen Sheldon. She's been here two years. Any questions you have she can answer them."

They stopped at one of the doors. The number twenty-two was painted in large red letters underneath a small viewing hatch. The guard knocked once but didn't wait for a response. She pushed the heavy door open and a wave of stale, tepid air hit Alice in the face. The room was square with a small, sealed window half-way up the wall opposite. There was a thin, brown carpet covering the floor and a narrow bed down each side. To the right of the door were a desk and a chair. No other furniture. A large, stooped girl was sitting on one of the beds. Her skin was red and blotchy and her dark, centre-parted hair hung down over her face. She didn't look up.

"Sheldon, this is Alice Vandella. Your new roommate." The guard waited. Then snapped, "Sheldon. Look at me when I'm addressing you."

The girl, Karen, slowly moved her head to take them in. If she was worried about upsetting the guard, she didn't let it show. She looked Alice up and down. Her eyes were so dark Alice couldn't see where the iris ended, and the pupil began.

The guard sniffed. "I'll leave you girls to get acquainted." She looked at her watch. "Dinner will be in an hour. Sheldon will show you what to do. Won't you?"

Karen didn't answer. The guard tutted loudly and then

shut the door, leaving Alice standing in the middle of the room not knowing what to do.

She smiled. "Hello." Her voice sounded meek and small. It annoyed her. "I'm Alice."

Karen lay back on her bed and put her feet up. "Yeah, I know. Vicky just said." Her voice didn't fit her body. It was high-pitched. Childlike.

Alice shuffled over and sat on the bed opposite. She bounced up and down, testing the springs. The way people did. It didn't seem too bad.

She looked across at Karen. She had her eyes closed and was breathing heavily down her nose, sending a clear message: don't talk to me. Well, that suited Alice fine. She rolled over on the bed and faced the wall as a tear rolled down the side of her nose and into her mouth. She tasted salt but made no move to wipe it away.

This was her life now. She had to accept it.

TWO

ALICE WOKE WITH A START TO FIND KAREN SITTING ON THE edge of her bed watching her.

"Jesus." She sat bolt upright, bringing her knees up to her chest.

Karen didn't flinch. "What you in for?" she asked, but Alice didn't answer. She wasn't sure how much she should tell people. "Woah. What's that all about? Your eyes," Karen asked. "They're mental."

Alice stared into Karen's black eyes. She could say the same. "I was born like this," she whispered. "One blue eye, one brown eye. Like David Bowie."

Karen wrinkled her nose. "Who?"

Alice shook her head. "Doesn't matter."

She thought of her mum. The evenings they'd spent together, listening to her old records. Back when life was simpler. How she wished she was back home right now, and those men had never started coming around.

"I tried to drown my baby sister," Karen said, matter-of-factly. "She survived. But they said I was a danger to myself and others. I also drowned the cat. He didn't survive." She looked at Alice. "I like to drown things."

Alice smiled. She wasn't sure why. Fear, maybe? Karen carried on staring at her without blinking and Alice got the impression she wasn't going to go until she'd told her the full sorry tale.

"I killed someone," she said. "But I didn't mean to. Well, I did. I don't know. He hurt my mum. I thought he'd killed her. I just snapped."

Karen looked impressed. "Murder? Fuck. That's huge. We've only got a few murderers in here. Did you enjoy it?"

Alice baulked at the question, unsure what to say. Unsure what the true answer was. She settled on a simple, "No."

"You'll have to be careful." Karen got off Alice's bed and stood in the middle of the room. "Once everyone finds out you killed someone, they're going to want a piece of you."

Alice frowned. "Why?"

"Way it is in here. They don't like people getting too big for their boots."

"I'm not proud of it." She swung her legs over the side of the bed and put her feet on the floor. "I had to do it."

Karen picked at her fingernail. "Don't matter. Murder puts you up there. They won't like that. Susan won't. Big Ella won't."

"Who?"

Karen beamed at her. "You'll find out soon enough, don't worry."

A buzzer sounded in the corridor. Piercing and loud.

Alice almost fell off the bed. "What the hell?"

It went again. Impossible to ignore. "Dinner," Karen said. "Come on."

They vacated their room and Alice followed Karen down the long corridor towards the canteen where they encountered a girl coming the other way. She was nearly six feet tall with strawberry blonde hair pulled back tight against her head in a short ponytail. Her eyes and lips looked puffy and watery, as though she'd been underwater for a long time. Karen looked at the floor and nudged Alice as the girl got nearer. Alice followed her lead. The girl snorted at them as she passed but didn't speak.

When she was out of earshot Karen whispered, "That was Susan. One of the ones I told you about."

Alice looked over her shoulder. She had been wondering. Though from the girl's size she'd assumed Big Ella. They got to the end of the corridor and went through another set of doors. It felt to Alice like they'd been walking for ages. Longer than when she'd arrived. The corridors all looked the same. There wasn't any daylight, or posters, or any hint of colour. For a place calling itself a home it sure felt a lot like a prison.

Karen pushed open the doors to the canteen and Alice followed through behind her. The room was noisy. What seemed like hundreds of girls milled around all wearing the same grey-on-grey outfit. A long line stretched around the perimeter of the room, all of them waiting for their turn at the serving hatch. Each girl held a small grey tray, divided up into smaller compartments. The ones already eating were sitting down, eight to a table. They talked, laughed, shouted at each other, but seemed well-behaved enough. Though as Alice scanned the room she reasoned the four guards - one in each corner - might have more sway than any real sense of civility.

"Get a tray and get in line," Karen told her. She picked up two trays and handed one to Alice. "You normally have to wait a while. It gets busy. Especially dinnertime. But the food's pretty good."

A stocky girl barged past them, then doubled back. She got up close to Karen. Too close. "We all know you like the food. Fat bitch." Karen looked down. She didn't respond. The girl moved her attention to Alice. "You're new, aren't you? What's your name?"

Alice glanced at Karen. "It's Alice. Alice Vandella," she replied. "I arrived this afternoon."

The girl screwed her mouth to one side. "Look at them eyes. Freak. You're the girl who killed that guy aren't ya? With the wine bottle." The girl glared at her. She had short black hair. Curly around her face. She was about an inch shorter than Alice, but her body was broad and thick. Like a barrel. "Hey, I'm talking to you freak."

Alice didn't answer. Didn't know what to say.

"Leave her alone," Karen said. "She's just settling in."

"Shut it fatty," the girl snapped. "Why don't you go drown yourself? Do us all a favour."

"Maybe I will," Karen replied.

The girl ignored her, jutting her face at Alice. "Do ya think you're hard, do ya?" She had thick eyebrows that met over the bridge of her wide nose. With her red face and downturned mouth, it made her appear permanently angry. She grabbed Alice by the collar of her sweatshirt. "I fucking run this place. All right? Bitch. Watch yourself."

Alice looked over at the guard. She was staring straight

at them. Watching. Doing nothing. Alice bowed her head. "I get it," she said. "I don't want any trouble."

The girl pushed Alice away. "I'll leave you two lezzas to get your dinner." She walked off, swinging her hips. Alice watched her walk down the line. Noticed how all the girls visibly tensed as she passed.

"I take it that was Big Ella?" she said to the back of Karen's head.

"Yeah." She glanced back, hiding behind her lank hair. "She's bad news. Worse than Susan. Stay away from her if you know what's good for you."

"I will," Alice said.

Karen sniffed. "Don't show any fear though. That's even worse. You need to stand up for yourself. But not so it'll piss her off. It's a mind field."

Alice was going to correct her. Tell her the term was 'minefield'. But she thought better of it. Maybe 'mind field' was more apt anyway.

"All I want is to get through the next few years as easy as possible," she told her. "Focus on getting out - back to normal." She held her tray to her chest.

Karen made a weird noise in the back of her throat. "Don't we all. But it isn't like that. You don't get to choose how easy you have it in here. People have heard about you. About what you did."

Alice peered over at the guard. The one who'd seen Big Ella confront her just now. She was still staring at Alice. Looking down her nose.

"I told you. I'm not proud of it," she whispered. "I promised my mum - the review people too - I'm going to keep my head down. Stay busy. Stay out of trouble."

Karen tucked a strand of hair behind her ear. "That'd be fine if the system wasn't rigged. But it is. Always has been." She spoke like she'd been inside for twenty years. Longer than she'd been alive. "People want you to fail Alice. They want you to mess up."

"Well, I'm not going to."

"Not so easy, though." They were nearly at the serving hatch now and Karen side-stepped along as she spoke. "Jabba wants you to fail. The screws want you to fail. The other girls certainly do. You can pretend this isn't happening to you. But it is. You might have been a nice little girl on the outside. All pretty, with your weird eyes and shit. But that isn't who you are any longer. You're never going to be that person again."

Alice had a sudden urge to shove her tray into Karen's neck, but she ignored it. "How do you know?" she asked.

"I just do. You can't stick your head in the sand and expect to get through this. You have to fight for your life in here. So, accept who you are now, Alice. Otherwise, you aren't going to survive."

Alice waved her away, she was trying not to listen. In the same way she'd tried not to engage too much with anything that had happened to her in the last three months: the court case, the remand centre, arriving at the home.

It was easier that way. Karen might have been inside longer and reckoned she knew it all. But she was weak. Alice could see that. She was also wrong. Alice wasn't sticking her head in the sand. Far from it. She was building a fortress around herself.

THREE

It was in the shower block, over a week later, when Alice saw the two girls again, together this time. She'd finished washing and was drying herself in the changing area when they appeared in the doorway.

For the past week, Alice had used the shower first thing and was dressed and back in her room before most of the other girls were even awake. But today was the first time since she'd arrived Karen hadn't woken her at the crack of dawn singing along to the Spice Girls, so Alice had slept in. It was now gone nine and the shower unit was packed. Though most of the girls quickly gathered their things together and scurried away as Big Ella and Susan prowled through the steam.

"Here she is. Freak eyes," Big Ella snarled. "You been avoiding us?"

"No," Alice said. She wrapped her towel around herself and looked through her pile of clothes. Searching for her knickers. "I've just not seen you."

Susan and Big Ella moved around so they were standing

on either side of her. Susan leaned against the wall, watching as Alice located her knickers and carefully stepped into them, pulling them up under the towel.

"What's it feel like, killing someone?" Susan asked. It was the first time Alice had heard her speak but her voice sounded exactly as she'd imagined. Nasal. Like she was bunged up with snot. "Did it turn you on?"

Alice picked up her bra from the pile and turned it around in her hands. "No. Course not. I don't remember it to be honest."

"I heard you cut the guy's head off." Big Ella said, her eyes widened.

Alice shook her head. "I don't remember." She held the bra in front of her for another few seconds. She had to remove the towel.

"How can you not remember?" Susan asked. She stared at Alice's chest as she dropped the towel and quickly pulled the sports bra over her head. "If I'd stabbed someone so many times their head came off, I reckon I'd remember it."

Alice looked at the ceiling.

"Hey, freak. Don't be a dick." Big Ella reached up and slapped Alice's right breast. It stung. "We're only interested. Aren't we Sue?"

The pain had focused Alice. She felt the pressure in her head. The fluttering of something in her stomach and chest. Her fists tightened.

She turned to the two girls and considered them a moment. They were tough, sure. Both of them together would be a struggle. But Alice had fought larger and meaner opponents in last year's Judo championship. Fought them and beat them. She was stronger than she looked. She took a deep breath. No. She'd promised herself as much as she had her mum. She'd keep her head down. Stay busy. Stay out of trouble.

She pulled on her jogging bottoms and grabbed her vest. "Sorry," she told them. "I don't know what you want me to say. I didn't mean to do it."

"Why did you then?"

She put the vest on. "He'd hurt my mum. I thought he'd killed her." She trailed off and pulled the sweatshirt over her head.

The girls carried on staring. Trying to scare her. Psyche her out. Alice knew the signs. She certainly didn't feel comfortable in this place, but she wasn't so naive she hadn't experienced life. She'd grown up in South London. Gone to a rough comprehensive. She'd seen things. Done things. She only looked innocent.

"You think you're better than all the rest of us, don't ya?" Big Ella squinted at her.

Alice shook her head. "No. honestly. Please. I don't."

"Have you fucking heard her. Like she's some princess."

Susan mimicked Alice. Over-egging it as though she was some simpering prima donna. Then, before Alice knew what was going on she'd slammed a fist into the side of her face.

Alice stumbled into the wall. Susan had caught her under her eye socket. Right on the cheekbone. A rush of adrenaline shot through her system. Awakening something inside of her. It took all Alice's focus to stay calm. To remember her promise.

"Come on," Susan spat. "Fight back, you dumb bitch."

Big Ella was in her other ear, pushing at her. "Let's have it."

Alice closed her eyes and pushed past them. The pressure in her head was unbearable. Like a thousand tiny voices screaming across her nervous system. She counted to ten as she darted to the door, anticipating another attack. A blow to the back of the head. Or worse. But it didn't arrive. They let her go.

"Watch yourself, slag."

She got to the door of the shower unit and saw Karen waiting for her.

"You all right?" she asked.

Alice rushed past her into the corridor. She could still hear Susan and Big Ella calling after her, calling her every horrible name under the sun, but she kept on walking. She didn't stop or raise her head until she got to room twenty-two.

FOUR

ALICE DIDN'T RECEIVE ANY VISITORS FOR THE FIRST THREE months of her stay in Crest Hill. This was mainly down to the fact that, apart from her mum, she had no real family to speak of. Louisa - her mum - had been writing to her, and Alice had written back, but it wasn't the same. She was still in a lot of pain and unsteady on her feet, she told Alice in her letters, and still felt nervous being outside. Alice understood. They'd both been through a lot. Yet, as the days ticked away, and each Tuesday came around with no visit her heart began to ache.

It had gone on so long that when Janet poked her head around the door and informed Alice she had a visitor, she thought she was joking.

"Very funny."

"I'm serious. Your mum's here. I guessed it was your mum. She looks like you. Come on." She smiled. Janet was all right. The nicest of all the guards in Block C by a long shot. Though still not one to mess with. Fair is what she was. But that was all Alice wanted.

She followed along behind as Janet led her to the visitor's hall. Alice hadn't been this far out of her block since her first day here. Had no reason to. The journey was longer than she'd remembered but, eventually, Janet stopped outside a door before unlocking it and stepped aside.

"You been told the rules?" Alice shook her head. "No hugging. No touching of any kind. If she's got a care package for you then she'll give it to the duty guard who'll pass it on to you once inspected. That's about it."

"Thanks," Alice said. She paused. From where she was standing, she could only see a sliver of the room. Four tables. They were all occupied but none of the adults were her mum. She felt nervous suddenly.

"Go on then," Janet said. "She was late, so you've only got twenty minutes."

She put her hand on Alice's back and pushed her into the room. Alice blinked in her surroundings. Large windows ran the full length of the far wall. The most natural light Alice had seen in a long while. Outside the sun was bright. The trees had turned green since she'd been inside.

"Alice, my baby girl."

She looked across the room to see her mum. But who could miss her? She was wearing a bright red headscarf and large, cat's eye sunglasses, standing waving her arms around dramatically. Alice put her hand up to show she'd seen her, hoping she'd sit down and be quiet, but she kept on waving. As Alice shuffled over to her, she could sense all the other girls watching and snickering at her. As she got closer, she took in the rest of her mum's outfit - a skin-tight red dress that extenuated her full bust and a leopard print coat, draped over the back of her chair.

"How are you, my darling?" she gasped, as Alice got nearer. She reached out and pulled her close.

Alice froze. "We're not allowed to hug." She whispered. "Let's sit, okay?"

Her mum pulled a face but did as she was told. She took off her sunglasses and leaned forward. "Oh crikey, Al. what happened to your face?"

Alice touched her eye. She'd forgotten about the bruise. Another run-in with Big Ella. This time in the games room. She'd thrown a table tennis bat at Alice and pretended to the guard it was an accident.

"It's nothing," she said. "I opened a door on it."

Her mum stared at her. Her face was stern. "Yeah. I've done that a few times myself."

A silence fell between them. Alice fiddled with her hands.

"Can we talk about something else?"

They made small talk for a while. Louisa told her how one of the neighbours' cats had got run over. Alice listened but her head felt heavy.

"Are you settling in all right?" her mum asked. "Made any friends?"

"It's not school mum."

"I know. I'm sorry I've not visited. I wasn't well. You know. And it's quite a trek up here."

Alice played with the stud in her ear. The only jewellery allowed in Crest Hill. "I understand. You catch the train down?"

Her mum looked away. Shook her head. "How then?"

"A friend brought me," she said. "He's waiting outside."

Alice was about to ask who, when she realised what that meant. "I thought you said you were going to stop all that."

"I was. I will. He's just a friend, Al. Promise."

A silence fell. Alice picked at the skin on her thumb but could feel her mum's eyes burning into her skull. Could feel the eyes of every girl in the room doing the same. Her skin was hot. Burning hot. She wanted to scream. To run away. To hide. Images flashed across her mind. She saw Big Ella, Susan. Saw herself slashing their necks open with a broken wine bottle.

"Sweetheart, are you listening to me?" She was back in the room. "Sorry, what?"

"I said I don't remember the last time I saw you smile."

Alice twisted her mouth to one side. "Not been much to smile about."

"I know, but we've talked about this. No looking back." Louisa moved her head, trying to make eye contact. "You hear me? What's done is done. We can't change that. But we can strive for better days, can't we? You'll be out of here in a few years. Still have your whole life in front of you." She put her hand over Alice's and squeezed. "Stay strong sweetie. Please."

A bell sounded.

"Five minutes everyone," the duty guard shouted. "Say your goodbyes."

Alice stood. "Right, well, see ya."

Her mum sulked. "Come on baby. Chin up. Please. I can't bear it."

That made two of them. "Will you be back again?" she asked.

"Course I will, sweetie. You try and stop me. It's your birthday soon, isn't it. I'll be back before then."

Alice frowned. "My birthday was two months ago. What are you talking about?"

Her mum's face was suddenly blank, as though she'd lost herself somewhere. Then she laughed and her eyes sparkled again. "Oh yeah. Silly me. Not sure what I was thinking. Just the stress of all this I suppose. Well, anyway. I'll be back soon. Promise."

Alice forced a smile. Though every time she did so it seemed to lengthen the distance between the action and any real emotion. "I'd best get back to my room," she said.

"You take care. I love you."

"Yeah. Same…you know."

Alice turned and shuffled back towards the door. She was hoping Janet would be there to meet her, but she wasn't. It was Julie. A shrivelled, bitter woman with a lop-sided mouth. She unlocked the door and Alice left the visitor's room and made her way once more down the long, dark corridor.

FIVE

ALICE HAD ALMOST REACHED HER BLOCK WHEN SHE NOTICED a girl up ahead, leaning with one foot against the wall where the corridor split into a T shape. To the right of her was the canteen and down to the left was Alice's block. As she got nearer, she could see it was the girl everyone in Crest Hill called Scrag. An acne-ravaged girl who hung about on the peripheries of Big Ella's gang.

She eyeballed Alice as she walked towards her. "That your ma, was it?"

Alice ignored her, headed for her block.

"Oi. Vandella." Scrag shouted after her. "I asked you a question. Was that your ma?"

Alice didn't look back. "Yes, it was my mum."

"Thought so. She a fucking slag then, or what?" Alice stopped. A ripple of heat energy shot down her arms. "She looks like one," Scrag went on. "My ma reckoned so too. Said she saw her getting dropped off by some old bloke in a Mercedes. That what she does? Suck off old blokes for money? Dirty whore."

Alice waited. Every muscle was taut. Her heart too. She felt tears forming in her eyes, but she didn't blink. Didn't turn around.

"I'm talking to you, bitch." Scrag was on her now. She grabbed Alice by the throat and slammed her against the wall. It caught her by surprise, but she didn't struggle. The pulsing pressure in her head was intense. The thoughts just as much.

"What the hell is going on? Let go of her." It was the guard, Julie. She scurried down the corridor towards them.

Scrag gave Alice's throat another squeeze and let go, pushing her back against the wall as she gasped for air.

"What do you think you're playing at?" Julie snapped. "Do you want me to send you both to the Governor?"

Scrag glared at Alice. "We were messing around. Weren't we?"

Alice rubbed at her neck. She couldn't speak even if she wanted to.

"Get to your rooms. Now," Julie snapped.

Alice let Scrag go first then made for her room as hot tears ran down her face. She got there and slammed the door behind her. Karen was sitting on her own bed listening to the Spice Girls on her pink ghetto blaster. Alice didn't make any effort to hide her tears. The world was crashing. Turning in on itself. She didn't know whether she wanted to scream or be sick or do cartwheels. She lay on her bed. Punched the pillow a few times. Didn't feel any better. Then she let the sobs come. Long and loud and unfiltered. Tearing out from her soul.

"Are you not feeling too good?" Karen asked once the sobs had died down.

Alice kept her head on the pillow but turned to look at her roommate, peering through the damp hair covering her eyes. "What gave it away, Karen?"

Karen turned the music off and screwed her nose up. "All this crying and shit. Thought you must be upset."

Alice sat up and wiped at her eyes. "Sorry. I feel like my heart might explode. Tough morning. And I've got all this prickly energy in my head and body."

Karen smiled knowingly and closed her eyes. "I get it. I feel like that sometimes. Usually, before I try and drown something. It helps me relax. Though I wouldn't recommend it. Not unless you want to stay in here forever."

"They want me to start with the therapist next week," Alice said. "Talk to some woman about my feelings and stuff. Do you have to go?"

"Yeah. It's stupid. But you get to sit in a comfy chair for an hour. It's a doss."

"That's what I thought," Alice said. "Stupid. I've got to see some sort of head doctor as well. They say what I did was so violent it might be a sign I've got, what was the word? Tendencies."

Karen turned her mouth down. "Yeah, they said that to me too. But you ask me we all have, don't we? That's why we're in here?" She pressed play on the ghetto blaster.

Alice groaned. "Don't you have any other music?"

Karen didn't look at her. "Spice Girls are my favourite. Why? What music are you into?"

"I like Bowie. Black Sabbath." Karen looked at her like she was speaking an alien language. "New York Dolls? Velvet Underground?"

Still nothing.

Alice lay back and closed her eyes. It was a new world she inhabited. Six months ago, she was a carefree teenager. Life was hard, sure. There were bits of it she didn't like to think about. All the male visitors for one. But she found solace in her music, and Judo, and her trampoline lessons. Plus, she was starting to get attention from the local boys. Had the whole world in front of her. Then that bastard did what he did, and everything changed.

Alice wasn't stupid. She knew what to say when they asked, these doctors. They wanted to hear her repent. Tell them how wrong it was, what she did. But that would be a lie. She turned over on her side and felt her body slowing down, the adrenaline leaving her system.

The problem was she couldn't repent, and she wasn't sorry. That man, Oscar Duke, deserved to die. The other girls in the remand centre called her a psychopath when she'd said that. And maybe they were right. The truth was she enjoyed killing the evil bastard. In the same situation, she'd do it again. Every single time.

SIX

"ARE YOU GOING TO EAT THAT?" KAREN ASKED HER.

"Excuse me?" Alice looked up from her tray where she'd been pushing a meatball around with her fork. "Oh, no. You have it if you want."

Karen leaned over and speared the greasy meatball with her fork. "You got your first session with Jacqueline this afternoon?" She stuffed the meatball in her mouth.

Alice put her fork down. "Does she ask loads of personal questions?"

"Nah," Karen spoke with her mouthful, bits of chewed-up meat spraying onto the table. "She just sits there most of the time. Stares at you. You don't have to say anything if you don't want to."

"I've to see Jacqueline and then a doctor," Alice told her. "They want to do tests on me, Jabba said. Mind tests. See what I think about things. I don't know. Sounds weird."

Karen swallowed the meatball. "Do they think you're a psycho?"

"Not sure."

"They thought I was. But I'm not. I have psychosis. It's not the same. Means I get confused and feel like the world is telling me to do to things. Drown things mainly." She picked at her teeth with her fork. "It's not my fault. Plus, I have tablets now. They help me feel normal. Most of the time anyway."

Alice smiled. It was a new world she was living in. But at least she had Karen. They would never have been friends on the outside, but here in Crest Hill, she was good to have around. She made Alice smile, even if most of the time it wasn't intentional.

Lunchtime was nearly over in the canteen and most of the girls had filed out. To play games or watch TV. The newest guard, Linda, waited for the stragglers. She was young and black and had kind eyes but a small, pursed mouth. Alice hadn't spoken to her much.

"You going straight to the medic block?" Karen asked. Alice looked at the clock above the serving hatch. "Nah,

got another hour yet. Might have a lie down. I've not slept properly the last few nights."

They both picked up their dirty food trays and stacked them in the large cabinets along the side wall.

"I'll come back with you," Karen said. "I can't be arsed watching TV. Neighbours will have finished. I'll watch the repeat later."

They'd left the canteen and were walking down the corridor when they heard footsteps behind them. Alice's senses were on overdrive. She knew who it was immediately. For weeks she'd existed in a state of calm alertness. Ready to act if needed. It was bolstering, but so tiring.

"Well look who it is," a voice sneered. Big Ella. Alice

sensed there were others too. Susan, from the sound of her footsteps. Maybe another. Scrag, perhaps. Alice and Karen kept on walking. Down to the end of the corridor and a left turn towards their block.

"Hey, Freak Eyes. Fatty Spice. Come here. Now."

Their pursuers had quickened their pace and were right behind them. Alice felt a hand on her shoulder. She stopped and turned around. Karen too.

"What do you want Ella?" Karen asked. "We're going back to chill."

"I want to speak to this bitch," Big Ella spat, eyeballing Alice. "Want to hear about her mum. I hear she's a slag. A prozzie. That true Freak?"

Alice stood her ground as Big Ella got so close their noses were almost touching. The girls weren't allowed perfume in Crest Hill, but Alice could smell it on her. It made her eyes sting. Sickly sweet. It didn't fit.

"Leave me alone," Alice told her. "I don't want any trouble."

"Oh, did you hear that, girls?" Big Ella snarled, spit flying from her mouth. "Freak Eyes don't want no trouble. You're a dirty slag. Just like your ma."

"Leave it will ya," Karen snapped pushing the bullies away. "She's not going to fight you. Piss off."

"What's that, Fat Spice? Are you feeling tough?" Ella neared on Karen and pushed her forehead against her chin. "Let's have it then?"

Alice bowed her head. Remembered her promise. She grabbed the sleeve of Karen's sweatshirt, meaning for them to walk away. But then Karen stepped forward and head-butted Big Ella.

"Oh, shit." Alice gasped as Big Ella's nose made a crunching sound and she stumbled against the wall. Karen was tall and she had brawn behind her. That would have hurt.

Susan and Scrag rushed to Big Ella's side and held her up. All the while shouting abuse. Playing the victim card, the sure-fire play of the bully. Blood gushed from Big Ella's nose.

"Hey! What the hell's going on here?" Linda's voice echoed down the corridor as she marched towards them. "You know you aren't supposed to be congregating here." As she got nearer, she saw Ella's with her head tipped back. Saw the blood. "What happened? Who did this?"

"It's nothing ma'am," Ella told her, holding the bridge of her nose. "I slipped and banged it. The girls here were helping me." She fought back tears.

Linda didn't look convinced. "Is that right?"

"Yes, ma'am," they all answered, in unison.

"Okay well, back to your rooms then. Ella, come with me. We'll get that looked at by the nurse."

Big Ella groaned but followed on behind as Linda strode purposefully back in the opposite direction. Before she turned the corner she looked back at Alice and Karen.

"You're dead," she whispered, at Karen. "Dead fucking meat."

Her cronies followed on behind her, both looking daggers at Karen as they backed up the corridor.

When they'd disappeared, Alice turned to her friend. "You okay?" she asked.

"Fine." Karen nodded. Her face was hard and emotionless.

"Aren't you worried they'll retaliate?"

"Let them," she said. "I'm not scared of those losers."

She looked at Alice and her face relaxed. Back to the Karen she knew. "It's like I told you, Al. You've got to stand up for yourself in here if you're going to survive. It's the only way. Otherwise, you'll drown."

Her eyes sparkled a second at the thought. Then she set off back to their room. Alice watched her for a few moments, feeling something like awe. Or gratitude. Or maybe it was plain old unease. She'd felt so many new emotions since being here it was hard to tell. She took a deep breath, unclenched her fists, and followed on behind. Maybe talking it out with this Jacqueline person would help after all.

SEVEN

THE WALLS OF THE THERAPY ROOM WERE PAINTED OFF-WHITE
- like every other wall in Crest Hill - but Jacqueline had tried
to make the room look a little less officious. There were
framed posters of waterfalls and rainbows, of serene lakes
and majestic horses running along beaches. All of them with
anodyne slogans and motivational quotes, written white on
black at the bottom.

Be your best self today.

You are only competing with yourself.

Happiness comes from within

Alice took it all in and shook her head. The same sneer
hadn't left her face since she walked into Jacqueline's room
ten minutes earlier. Ten minutes and they still hadn't got
going. Is this what therapy was all about?

Jacqueline rifled through some papers at the other side
of the room. "Just one minute, then I'll be with you," she
glanced up at Alice. "Do you want a glass of water or
anything?"

"No thanks."

"Okay. One minute."

Alice watched Jacqueline as she scan-read the notes in a brown file. Alice's file. The therapist's eyes flitted around the page, but her face showed no sign of concern. Or fear. Alice was watching for it. She had a knack for reading people. Always had. She could pick up on exactly what people were going to say, or do, most of the time. It was those heightened senses of hers, the chattering energy on the edge of her awareness. It was a help. Sometimes.

Jacqueline was in her late thirties. Glamorous, for a therapist. Though she was the first one Alice had ever met. The first one she'd ever seen in the flesh. Before entering the room today she'd imagined Jacqueline to be an old hippy. The beads and tie-dye variety. Jacqueline however was wearing black leggings and a black satin blouse. She wore her dark hair in a thick fringe, that gave her an air of some singer from the sixties. Not one in particular, she just looked cool.

"All right, sorry about that, let's begin, shall we?" Jacqueline sat down in the chair opposite Alice and closed her eyes. She took a deep breath, held it, then made a show of blowing out. "Can you do this with me?" she asked. "Gets us focused on the session. Three deep breaths. In and out. It helps ground us in the moment. Try it. It feels good."

Alice did as she was told. Although it was very much a half-arsed version of what Jacqueline was doing. Once they'd done the ritual three times Jacqueline opened her eyes and smiled. "So then, here we are. Alice Vandella. Such a great name by the way. Is it Italian?"

"Thanks," Alice mumbled, feeling her cheeks burn. "And yes. It is. My mum is from San Marino originally."

"Beautiful. Well, first things first," Jacqueline went on. "I want you to know this is a safe space. You can say whatever you want. I don't report back to anyone. Whatever you say in these four walls stays between me and you. That's it. Do you have any questions?"

Alice shrugged. "Not really."

Jacqueline nodded reassuringly. "Great. Why don't we start today by you telling me what happened? In your own words."

Alice titled her head to one side. She wasn't expecting this so soon.

"You mean why I'm in here?"

"That's right," Jacqueline said.

"I don't know. I mean, what do you want me to say?"

"Whatever you want to, Alice. This is your forum. I thought it would help for me to hear what happened from your perspective. Not from reports or police notes or anything like that."

She smiled sweetly and Alice realised she was already starting to trust her. But that worried her as much.

She took another deep breath and held it in her chest. Bracing herself for something. She wasn't quite sure what. But an energy bubbled inside of her, desperate to be released. Maybe this was the time?

"Where do you want me to start?" Alice asked. "Anywhere you want. Why don't you tell me about your mum?"

Alice frowned. "Isn't that like a real cliché?"

"Maybe it is for a reason." Jacqueline leaned forward, fake whispering. "I think the whole mum thing is only relevant for young boys though." She made a face and despite herself, Alice let out a soft giggle. But it faded quickly as she fell into her story.

"My mum looks after us," she began. "Any way she can. She was a dancer. But she hurt her leg. So she had to stop. We struggled after that. Had to move a few times. Then I don't know how it happened, but she started seeing this guy. Robert. He was all right. Most of the time he'd come over after I was in bed. I found out later he was married. He'd started paying my mum. To have sex with her."

She paused and looked out the window. She hadn't planned on saying any of this. She hadn't planned on saying anything. She couldn't see anything but sky through the small window. It was grey and overcast. The room remained silent. Jacqueline wrote something down in her notepad but offered no reply. They sat for a few minutes, meeting each other's gaze every so often. Alice wiped a tear from her eye. She had more to say.

"More men turned up. I don't know, word must have got out or something. My mum's never been short of men liking her. She's good-looking, for a mum." She wiped away another tear. Jacqueline smiled but still didn't speak. "It was fine though. In a way. Things between me and her weren't any different. But now we had a bit more money. Were more stable. Then one day I arrived home and he was there in the kitchen. First time I met him. Oscar Duke. I can see him even now. Sitting there, drinking my mum's whisky. He had a mean face. I remember he looked me up and down when I walked in. Like he was undressing me or something. Dirty old perv."

Jacqueline nodded slowly. There was a pause. "Did he ever touch you?" she asked, softly.

Alice shook her head. "No. But I wouldn't have put it past him. He wanted me to know he was looking though. Do you know what I mean? Wanted power over me. Fucking horrible bastard. Sorry."

"It's okay. As I say, this is a safe space. You can say whatever you want in here, Alice."

"Well, he was. I hated him from the start. Knew he was horrible. To think of him being all naked and gross on top of my mum." She shuddered. Her hands gripped tight to the arms of the chair. "Then the bruises started. The cuts and stuff. I never saw him hit her, but I heard him shouting, breaking stuff. I used to put my Walkman on as loud as I could to drown it all out. Then one day I came back from school, and he was in the kitchen."

She stopped. Her voice breaking as she spoke. Tears fell fast from her eyes, and she wiped her nose on her sleeve. She was annoyed. She'd promised herself she'd stay calm. Stay strong. Just like she'd promised herself she'd keep her head down and get through the next few years without any trouble. Two promises she was still determined to keep.

Alice looked up at the clock over Jacqueline's shoulder. She had fifteen minutes left of the session. The time had flown by.

"We can leave it there if you want. There's no rush."

Alice shook her head. "No. I want to say it. I want to say what he did."

She'd been carrying the pain inside of her for too long. It was like a horrible gremlin. Laughing at her. Mocking her any time she felt a spark of hope. Maybe if she spoke about it all that torment would subside. That was her hope. That's why she was here.

"The next thing I saw was my mum on the kitchen floor." She sniffed. "Actually no. that's not true. It was the blood. A big pool of it. It was all up the walls. Across the tiles. Then I saw my mum. I thought she was dead, I really did. He was standing over her and had been…attacking her. With a wine bottle. The sick fuck." She paused. Blew out her cheeks. Looked at the clock. Five minutes to go. "I can't remember what happened next. I think I launched myself at him. Surprised him. Knocked him into the wall. I'm stronger than I look. He fell. Dropped the bottle. Then I was on him."

She stopped again. Her heart felt like it was going to erupt out of her throat. One minute left. There was no time. She swallowed. She shook her head. Shook the images away. Tried at least.

"Can we talk about this later?" she asked.

"Of course," Jacqueline said. "Shall we leave it for today?"

"Yes please."

"Good work though Alice. You're right. You're a lot stronger than you look. Got great emotional intelligence too, I'd say. That will fare you well."

Alice pondered the statement. She wasn't sure what it meant. She knew she was clever. She always had been, even if she'd played it down most of her life. You didn't survive long at the schools she'd attended if you were a swot.

"Is that it then?"

"Yes. But I'll see you same time next week," Jacqueline leaned forward and gripped her by the knee. "Thank you for today, Alice." The clock hit the hour and, right on time, there was a knock on the door. Linda, here to escort her to her next appointment. Jacqueline stood up. "I believe you're seeing Dr Richards next. Don't worry. She can be a little cold, but she's on your side. Just wants to help. Remember that."

Alice stood up as Linda opened the door and beckoned her out. Her legs felt wobbly, and she stamped them out as she moved to the door. She worried Dr Richards would find something wrong with her. Give her pills. Like they had done with her mum. But Alice knew, there was nothing wrong with her pills could solve. They gave you pills because you couldn't cope with life. As though you were the problem. But Alice knew, life was the problem. It was always had been.

EIGHT

As it turned out Dr Richards was a far cry from the Nazi-scientist-type Alice had imagined. She was a large African woman with a strong accent and a stern manner. But she spoke truthfully and honestly, and Alice appreciated that. The session started with Dr Richards asking her general questions about her life. Her interests, whether she liked to exercise. Then she moved on to more pressing matters. How she felt about what had happened, about what she'd done. Her time so far in the home.

Alice answered as honestly as she could but swerved any questions relating to her moods. Her mind was strong. She knew that. With focus that dark energy - always there at the corners of her consciousness – could be valuable. Useful, even. It had been in the past. In her Judo competitions. Even with her schoolwork. It was a feeling of super-creativity, coupled with an extreme sense of invincibility. She couldn't risk numbing that energy.

So, when Dr Richards asked Alice told her what she wanted to hear. That she felt fine. That she was sorry for what she'd done, and in her opinion, it was a spur-of-the-moment act, triggered by what she'd seen - and what she thought Oscar Duke might do to her next. It was self-defence. But of course, she continued, she completely understood if you killed someone, even in self-defence, you had to be punished. Had to do the time.

Alice wasn't entirely sure Dr Richards believed everything she told her. Especially as the same dark energy had been swelling inside of her the whole time. She'd spoken quickly and at length, her eyes darting around as she took in the medical facility, assessing the situation in real-time.

The doctor seemed satisfied however - once she'd weighed and measured Alice and taken some blood – that all was well. For now. She'd see Alice in a few months she said. Would continue to monitor her. A good show all round, Alice thought as Linda arrived to take her back to her room.

Karen was lying on her bed singing along to the Spice Girls when Alice arrived back. No surprises there.

"Don't you listen to anything else, Kaz?" she asked as she slumped down on her own bed.

Karen stopped singing and looked at Alice like she was crazy.

"Why would I? They're the best band in the world. Better than that depressing shit you listen to. Bloody Goth music. Weirdo."

Alice grinned. She'd heard it all before. She also wore the disdain like a badge.

"Jacqueline's all right, isn't she?"

"Told you you'd like her." Karen got up and changed

the CD. More Spice Girls. A different album. Alice didn't know there was more than one. "Do you fancy her?"

Alice pulled a face. "What? Get lost. No."

Karen climbed back onto her bed. "Lot of the girls do in here. That's all. And she's like you, isn't she? All dark and gothic and slinky."

"Slinky?"

"You know. Athletic or whatever. Skinny bitches."

She looked at Alice and they both burst out laughing. It wasn't so bad being in here, Alice realised. Freedom was an issue, but she'd made her peace with that. Prior to killing Oscar Duke, she had been going off the rails. Maybe this was what was supposed to happen. An enforced penance to get her back on track. Keep her away from the chaos of the outside world. Jacqueline was nice, and whilst Alice would never admit it out loud, she'd enjoyed her first therapy session. Something inside had lifted. For now at least she felt calm.

NINE

ALICE WOKE UP AND LOOKED AROUND HER. THE SUN WAS already up and shining brightly through the small window. It bounced off one of Karen's CDs, reflecting flashes of rainbow light onto the wall above Karen's bed, but she was nowhere to be seen. Alice sat up and picked up the alarm clock, narrowing her sleepy eyes at the reading. The red numbers glared out at her. Seven-thirty. She'd slept in. For once. That wasn't like her. Maybe the therapy was already working.

She swung her legs over the side of the bed and padded barefoot over to the window. They were on the ground floor, but the only window was long and narrow and positioned in a way that all she could see were tree tops. They were green and luscious. Spring was here, and despite everything, it gave Alice a renewed vigour. She might even call it hope.

Karen's bed was unmade, but that was normal. Alice sat down on the edge of it and felt the recess in the pillow. Felt the sheets. They were cold. Karen must have left at least

40

half an hour earlier. Maybe more. It was odd. Alice usually had to wake her up.

Alice pulled on her jogging bottoms and a vest top and opened the small cupboard unit each girl had at the end of their bed. She took out her towel, and the shampoo and conditioner her mum had sent the week earlier. Flashing anything new or expensive-looking around in this place was dangerous, so Alice spent a few minutes peeling the labels from both bottles. Then she wrapped the towel around them and set off for the showers.

The block was down two long corridors and through two large fire doors, but Alice had only travelled down the first corridor when she heard a commotion. There were shouts and laughter, and the sound of people running up and down. Through the next fire door and down to her left she could see flashing lights coming from the visitor's car park.

Alice quickened her pace. Outside the door to the shower block, a large crowd had gathered. Mostly inmates, but there were guards here too. Alice could even see Jabba walking around. She looked stern - which wasn't unusual - but there was something else there behind her eyes, Alice could see. Concern. Worry. Sorrow, even.

Alice scurried faster down the corridor. Past two policemen, mumbling into walkie-talkies. She didn't catch what they said, but the looks on their faces told her it was serious. She got up to the fringe of the crowd and peered over the heads of the other girls. She was only average height - around five-four barefoot - so it was hard to make out what was going on. On her tiptoes, she saw two ambulance workers wheel something into the shower block.

"Hey, Mary. What's happening?" Alice asked.

Mary was a tall, Irish girl with jet black hair. She'd been in Crest Hill coming up to five years and knew the lay of the land.

She turned to Alice and her eyes widened. "Shit, don't ya know? I thought you were with her?"

Alice shook her head. "Know what? Oh shit. No."

"Aye. Karen. She's dead love. Some of the girls found her this morning. About an hour ago. Face down in the large bathtub. Drowned."

Alice's skin went cold. She felt like she was going to be sick.

"How? Who did it?" she asked.

"No one's singing. But we both know who did it. Don't we? Especially after what Karen did to Big Ella. Gave her a right shiner she did."

Alice left Mary and pushed her way through the crowd of girls. She had to hear it for herself. The pressure in her head was back. The chattering too. She clenched her fists as she went. Wanted to kill every single person here. Smash their stupid dawdling heads against the wall.

"Get out the fucking way," she yelled, elbowing through the throng.

She got to the entrance of the showers at the same moment the two ambulance workers reappeared. They wheeled out a stretcher with a body under a sheet.

"Aw, no. No." Alice rushed at the stretcher and pulled back the starched white sheet. It was Karen all right. Her face was more bloated than normal. Her expression frozen into a terrified scream. The skin around her face was puffed up and blue and her eyes bulged out of their sockets.

Alice stared down as her heart broke once more. Time stopped. Then she felt arms around her chest, hands on her shoulders, pulling her away. Then voices. Lisa maybe. Jabba. "Come on girl, let them do their job. There's nothing you can do."

One of the guards guided Alice away. She felt numb. Like the world had suddenly shifted and she was unsure how to behave. How to function. They'd killed Karen. Those vindictive bitches had killed Karen. And for what? A tussle about nothing. A black eye. The darkness swelled in Alice's soul.

They were going to pay for this.

They all were.

"Alice? Are you listening to me?" The world swam back into focus. Linda was in her face, a look of deep concern on hers. "Do you want to see Jacqueline? She's available."

Alice thought. "No. I want to be on my own." She looked up at Linda. "Is that okay? Please?"

Linda looked over her shoulder. "I've been told to keep an eye on you. Just until we know what's going on."

"What's going on?" Alice mimicked. "My friend has been killed. I think we know what's going on, Linda. I think we all know who did it as well."

Linda looked away. She was a coward, Alice thought. Just like the rest of them. A jobsworth. She didn't care about Karen, or her. No one did.

"Can I go to my room, please?" she asked Linda. "I swear, I'll stay there."

Linda tutted, but she was thinking about it. "All right, I'll escort you back. But don't do anything stupid, Alice. You hear me? In fact, I'm going to lock you in until things have calmed down."

Alice sighed. "Fine. I want to be on my own."

They made their way back to Alice's room in silence. Linda shut the door quietly behind her and turned the key, leaving Alice standing in the middle of the room. She remained there for a good few minutes. Unable to move. Every muscle was stiff with rage. Her limbs bristled with nervous energy.

She walked over to Karen's bed and slumped down on the unmade sheets. The world had shifted, that was true. But so had she. Something inside of her had clicked into place. Without really thinking what she was doing she picked up the Spice Girls CD from the nightstand. She turned it around, seeing herself reflected in the shiny gold plastic – like a ghost, staring back at her. Her mouth was cruel. Her eyebrows furrowed. She looked like she'd aged ten years in one morning. Maybe she had.

She nodded to herself. She was ready now. Ready to face the future. Ready to do what was needed. To survive. But first she was going to make Big Ella and all her stupid miserable friends pay for what they did.

TEN

Alice saw Jacqueline a lot after Karen died. Her weekly sessions were doubled-up to include Thursdays as well as Tuesdays. It was standard practice she was told, if someone close to you died, to up the therapy sessions. That and being placed on suicide watch.

"So how are you feeling today?" Jacqueline asked once she'd gone through the usual rituals, settling Alice into the session.

"Bit confused. Upset. Sad. Angry as hell." As she spoke Jacqueline frowned and nodded along. The usual response. Weaponised silence. She waited for Alice to go on. She usually did. "I promised my mum - and myself - I'd get through this as easily as I could. Keep my head down. Be a good little girl. Whatever. But I realise now I can't keep that promise."

"I see. And what does that mean, Alice - you can't keep that promise?"

Alice picked at the skin on the side of her thumb. "Means I understand now what Karen was saying. I have to fight. I have to be strong, and I have to stick up for myself. Otherwise, I'm not going to get through this time inside."

She watched Jacqueline, hoping for some sort of sign. Despite herself, Alice trusted her therapist. Trusted whatever she said in here went no further. But still, she often wished Jacqueline would offer some sort of input. Now and again at least. Tell her what she should do. Or at least give an opinion. The problem was she was too damn neutral.

"Do you use the word, fight, metaphorically?" Jacqueline asked.

"Don't know… No… You see, I know who killed Karen. And eery one of the useless cows who work here knows as well. They just haven't got proof so they can't – or won't - do anything about it."

"They have to step careful—"

"Fucking cowards is what they are." Alice was on her feet. She caught herself in time and walked over to the window. It was a nice day outside. The sky a vibrant shade of soft blue, with a gentle smattering of cotton candy clouds. Alice placed her forehead against the glass and closed her eyes. The window was cold against her skin. Her head pounded. "Sorry," she whispered. "Maybe I'm not coping too well."

Jacqueline waited a minute before speaking. "Have you seen Dr Richards recently?"

Alice kept on looking out the window. "Yeah. She's useless. She gave me some pills. Said they'd help level out my moods." She turned back to Jacqueline. "But I threw them away."

Jacqueline nodded. "They might help you cope better."

"The way Dr Richards explained it - she said they'd shave off the top and bottom bits of my moods. Like I'd not feel so down but they'd also stop me feeling good. You see sometimes I feel amazing. Like I can take on the world. I don't want to lose that." She stopped, realising she'd been talking fast. She sat back down. Calmed herself. "Do you get what I mean though? I'd rather take the rough with the smooth. I don't want to sound like a twat, but I reckon I'm strong enough and clever enough to cope with the dark times. I don't want to dampen it down if it means dampening the good bits of me too."

Jacqueline didn't blink for a long time. She appeared to be thinking. Then she narrowed her eyes at Alice and smiled. "Interesting," is all she said. She picked up a notepad and wrote something down. "What happens now, Alice? In terms of this new decision - to fight. How does that work from day to day?"

Alice looked Jacqueline in the eyes. "I'm going to get revenge. For Karen. I'm going to show those rotten bitches they can't do that and get away with it."

Jacqueline stopped writing and looked up. "Alice, I need you to know - whilst we have a confidentiality clause in our sessions - if you disclose to me that your thinking of doing harm to yourself or others then that clause is void. I'll have to report it." Jacqueline's eyes sparkled in the fluorescent light but gave nothing away.

"Fine," Alice told her. "All I mean is I have to fight for my sanity. You know. Fight to keep who I am alive. That's all."

A smile teased at the corner of Jacqueline's mouth. She wrote something down. "I think that's a good way to think," she said. "You've got a lot going for you, Alice Vandella. I don't want you to ruin things for yourself."

Alice snorted. "What have I got going for me? Being stuck in this place? Labelled a psycho? My only friend dead?"

Jacqueline put down her pen. "Come now. I see a young woman with her whole life in front of her. She's bright, creative, witty - a little too cutting for her own good sometimes, but I like that." She tilted her head to try and make eye contact. "Not to mention you're an attractive girl, Alice. Not that it should matter. But it does. Those eyes of yours."

Alice bowed her head some more. She didn't want Jacqueline to see any hint of the smile she was forcing down. "They call me freak eyes."

"Do names bother you?"

Alice let the grin spread. "Nah. I like it to be honest. I like being a freak. Always have. Besides they're like Bowie's."

Jacqueline laughed. "You a fan?"

Alice nodded. "Yeah, he's great. My mum liked – likes - him. I grew up with him. She's got good taste in music has my mum."

"I'll say. Though you're wrong. They're not like Bowie's. Yours are different colours."

Alice frowned. "Yeah, so are his."

"No actually they're not," Jacqueline said. "Have a look again. They do appear that way but only because of trauma to one of his pupils. It's constantly dilated, so it looks darker. But his eyes are both blue." Alice was staring at her now. Jacqueline smiled. "I'm a big fan too. What's your favourite album?"

Alice paused, unsure whether this was some sort of therapist technique, to try to create more connection. She was, however, glad to be talking about something other than emotions and dead friends.

"The Man Who Sold The World," she replied. "Most days. The thing about Bowie is he changed his style so much there's an album for every one of your moods." She looked away, embarrassed suddenly at her comment. It dawned on her whether this was why she loved him so much. The warped, chameleon aspect of his persona. She could relate.

"Good choice," Jacqueline said not picking up on the comment or choosing to ignore it. "I'm more of a mid-period fan. It's Station to Station for me." She sat up, closed her notepad. "Anyway, thank you for today, Alice. As always I welcome your candidness."

Alice stood up. Her heart sank. Going back to her room after a session was never an exciting prospect, especially now she was on her own. Jabba informed her last week she'd be getting a new roommate, but it hadn't happened yet.

"I guess I'll see you Thursday then."

"Yes. Have a good week until then. And Alice - about what we said."

"Yes?" Alice was at the door but stopped and turned around.

Jacqueline stood and moved over to her. Speaking softly now. "I mean it. Anything you tell me regarding harming anyone, I will have to report. But that's not to say you shouldn't stand up for yourself. I'm not saying getting revenge for Karen is a good idea. But if you were to go down that path, my advice is to be clever about it. Don't let anger drive you. That won't help. And take them one by one."

Alice looked up at Jacqueline. Was she messing with her? Trying for some sort of confession?

She went on. "Remember, no one can punish you without evidence, Alice. Strike when no one else is around and slip away fast. Don't get caught."

She lay a hand on Alice's shoulder. Her face was cold. Serious. Then, as if a light went back on in her eyes, she smiled and opened the door.

"You take care of yourself, Alice, and I'll see you on Thursday. Be well."

With that, she gently pushed Alice out into the corridor and shut the door behind her.

What the hell?

Alice stood in the dark corridor a moment, unable to comprehend what had happened. Had she imagined it? Was this part of her craziness? She had a thought to go back in and have it out with Jacqueline, but before she had a chance Linda appeared. And with her head now swarming with questions Alice was escorted back to her room.

ELEVEN

It was a Sunday afternoon, two weeks later, when it happened. Alice had spent as much time as possible before then alone in her room. Preparing herself not only mentally for what was to come, but also physically. Sit-ups and push-ups mainly. Exercise had been a regular thing for her when she was on the outside but since being stuck in Crest Hill, she'd found it hard to motivate herself. She was still lithe, still had that athletic slinkiness Karen had mentioned, but she felt flabby. Felt it physically and mentally. And she needed both aspects of her to harden up.

She'd also begun punching the wall for a few minutes every hour or so. The walls here were made of painted breezeblocks and her knuckles throbbed and bled. But that was what she wanted. It was a technique she'd discovered after talking with Davinder, one of the older kids at Judo. He'd told her about this new sport called MMA, *Mixed Martial Arts*, which sounded to be a cross between Judo and boxing. But more brutal. He told Alice how continuous punching of hard surfaces created callouses on the hands, especially on the knuckles. A punch was then much more deadly. The skin was tougher but also the person punching could hit harder. Davinder reckoned he'd broken someone's nose without even feeling it. That was what Alice hoped for.

Her mum had sent her some CDs, after months of requests. Masters of Reality by Black Sabbath and Bowie's Station to Station. These become the soundtrack to Alice's training regime. She pounded the wall and bled for Karen as the Thin White Duke's insanity grew. Sabbath's proto-metal hymns patched her bruised soul back together.

Alice woke up Sunday morning refreshed and ready. She'd slept better than she had done in maybe two years. Since the time before Oscar Duke. Back when she was still a precocious but carefree teenager. A kid. It felt like a lifetime ago. It was Alice's sixteenth birthday in a week. Not that she planned on celebrating. Although, if she carried out what she had planned it would be cause for some celebration. In here you took what you could. Pyrrhic victories be damned.

"Not seen you in a while. How are you holding up?" Mary smiled at Alice as she took a seat next to her in the canteen.

"I'm doing all right," Alice told her. "Shit though, isn't it?"

For the first few days after Karen had been killed the guards had kept Alice locked in her room and had food brought to her. Later she'd sneaked here towards the end of service, knowing the queues would be quiet, most of the tables empty. It had suited her. She needed quiet. Room to think. To focus the frenzied energy swirling inside of her into something useable.

"Aye it is shit all right," Mary replied. "She wasn't a bad lass was she, Karen. Could be a real laugh."

Alice smiled in agreement, but she wasn't listening. She played around with the mash potatoes on her tray, picking up a large dollop on her fork and splattering it back down again.

"You sure you're all right?" Mary asked. "You seem different. Look different."

Alice ignored her. But she knew what she meant. She'd seen it in her reflection every day since she'd killed Oscar Duke, but it had accelerated since Karen's death. It wasn't a harshness exactly, but she looked older. More world-weary. When she was over-tired especially, her eyes could look damn scary, even to herself. It was like she was looking through you and wanted to kill you all at once. A thousand-yard stare, that's what Jacqueline had called it. Alice hadn't known what she meant at first but had looked it up in the library block. It was related to war veterans, people who'd experienced too much horror in combat, had seen too much of life. It made sense.

"I'm fine," Alice told Mary. "Keeping my head down. One day at a time."

The generic platitudes received the desired response. Mary shut up and ate. Alice waited.

Another thirty minutes and Big Ella appeared in the queue, along with Susan and Scrag. As usual. Alice tensed, forcing herself not to look over at them. Out of the corner of one eye, she saw them getting their lunches. They walked over to a table on the opposite side of the room. They were looking over and laughing, but once they'd settled down Alice stood up. Holding her tray in front of her, hands gripping the sides, she made her way over to the metal shelving unit that housed the dirty dinner trays

There was a large pile of mashed potato on her tray, along with a plastic beaker filled with water. At the shelving unit, Alice paused, psyching herself up, readying herself. The guard, Linda, was standing by the double doors - to the left of where Big Ella was sitting, with her back to Alice. It would take the guard two strides to get over to the table.

Alice took a deep breath and went for it, moving over to Big Ella's table. As she got closer, she faked a trip and tossed the mash potato and beaker of water all over Big Ella's head.

"Oh my god, you're a fucking mental bitch." She was up on her feet in a second. As were Susan and Scrag. They turned on Alice, fists raised, ready to fight. But Linda was between them in a flash.

"Calm it down, girls. I mean it," she yelled, pushing Big Ella back.

"I'm so sorry," Alice yelped. "It was an accident. I think I must have slipped on some gravy or something." She gazed up at Linda, giving her the old Bambi eyes.

"I'm soaked through. Dickhead," Big Ella snarled. "You're dead Vandella. You hear me?"

"It was an accident," Alice tried again, appealing to Linda.

"I said calm it down," Linda snapped. "We don't want that sort of talk around here. Do we?"

Big Ella stepped back and pulled at her sweatshirt in disgust. "I can't sit here like this. I'll get pneumonia or something. Is that what you want?"

Linda looked panicked suddenly. Lunchtime was the

changeover period for the guards at Crest Hill, but sometimes those taking over the afternoon shift arrived late. Like today. It meant Linda was overseeing the whole of this block. It meant she couldn't leave her post.

"If you're really wet you can get a change of clothes from the laundry unit," she said. "But be quick. Straight there and back. Understand?"

Big Ella looked at Alice and snarled.

Alice looked at the floor. "I'm sorry," she muttered.

"It was an accident," Linda told her. "No harm done. Where are you going now, Vandella?"

"Back to my room. I have a session with Jacqueline soon."

"Okay, good. Go there now please."

Alice nodded and made her way slowly out of the room. Behind her she could hear Linda telling Ella to go to the laundry unit straight away and come back to finish her lunch. She said she had five minutes or she'd come looking for her.

Alice smiled to herself as she left the canteen. Five minutes was all she needed.

TWELVE

Alice heard the doors open behind her as she made her way down the corridor to her room. It was Linda, checking she was going where she said she was. Without turning back, she kept on walking until she'd moved around the corner out of sight. Once there she stopped, hearing the doors swing open once more and Big Ella's voice.

"Dumb bitch."

She made a noise like she was kicking at the wall before shuffling up the corridor, no doubt on her way up to the laundry unit.

Alice lifted her sweatshirt and removed the fork she'd stuffed down the waistband of her jogging bottoms. Clutching it in her fist she double-backed on herself and silently followed Big Ella down to the end of the corridor. She had about twenty seconds after Big Ella turned the next corner where there were no rooms in earshot. That was her moment.

She eased her head around the wall and saw Big Ella dragging her heels, still pulling at her wet clothes. Then she stopped, as though listening for something. Footsteps? Alice froze and dipped back behind the wall. If she was seen before she had a chance to get close everything was ruined. Time stopped. Alice held her breath. A second went by. She risked peering around the wall to see Big Ella was pulling her sweatshirt off over her head. This was it.

In a second, she was on her. There was a reason she had the nickname "Big' Ella. She was at least a stone heavier than Alice and sturdy with it. But Alice had the element of surprise. She also had a demon inside of her. As Ella pulled the sweatshirt over her head and with her arms still wound up in the material, Alice struck. A swift punch to the windpipe took left Ella gasping in shock and confusion. As she stepped back, Alice grabbed her sweatshirt and pulled it back and behind her, taking her arms with it and leaving her open. Then with her teeth gritted in rage, she brought up the fork and stabbed it into Big Ella's eye.

"Argh—"

Her screams were caught short as Alice gripped a hand over her mouth and yanked her head back. She continued to gouge down with the fork, feeling the gelatinous gristle of her eyeball pop. Another half-inch and she'd be in Ella's brain. Another inch and she'd be dead.

But Alice didn't want that.

Not yet.

She pulled out the bent fork, moving to one side as blood and tissue spurted out from the wound.

Big Ella was in full fight or flight mode now, groaning and grunting and kicking out to try and get away. But with her arms caught up in her sweatshirt and Alice dancing and evading the blows she got nowhere. Alice hit her with a sharp jab to the throat before grabbing her by the hair. With all the strength she had she slammed her friend's killer's head against the wall. It made a soft thud against the cold breezeblock. Unsatisfying. Alice went again, harder this time and leaving a ring of blood on the wall. Panting with rage and filled up with adrenaline Alice let her drop to the floor, before stomping down on her head, kicking her in the chest and face, over and over. Doing it for Karen. For everyone Big Ella had ever hurt. And for herself. And for her mum. And for the rotten unfairness of it all.

Then she stopped.

The whole attack had taken less than a minute. She let the fork drop to the floor where it made a dull clang. Alice looked up and down the corridor. There was no one in sight but Linda would be coming to check on Big Ella any minute. Alice squinted down at her foe. Her nose was a mush of cartilage, her cheekbone splintered, her eye gone. Indeed, her whole head was swollen and sticky with blood and plasma. She looked to be dead. But Alice wasn't hanging around to find out. She turned around and walked steadily back the way she'd come. Down the next corridor, she opened the door to the cleaner's closet and slipped inside. She'd already tested the lock a few days earlier. She shut the door and watched through the keyhole. It was a tight space, only a metre or two square and it stank of bleach. As expected, a few seconds later she saw Linda stride purposefully past, on her way to find Big Ella. Alice gave it a beat and then let herself out, before running back to her room.

Once there she had only minutes to get changed into the pre-prepared clothes she had laid out under her bedclothes -

ones she'd stolen from the laundry room a day earlier. She removed the bloody items she was wearing and stuffed them under the pillow. Then she took out the bottle of mineral water she'd squirrelled away and gave her face and hands a decent wash, focusing on her fingernails especially. Satisfied she was clean and fresh she lay on her bed and put on the stereo.

Job done.

THIRTEEN

THE SPICE GIRLS WERE SINGING THE REFRAIN OF TWO Become One when Linda and Sarah-Jane burst into Alice's room a few minutes later. They looked around, scowling. Sarah-Jane scuttled over to Alice's bed.

"You been here a while?" she snarled. "Excuse me?" Alice asked.

"She was in the canteen," Linda moved over to Karen's empty bed and looked under the bed. "But she left before Ella."

Alice shifted on the pile of bloody clothes under her sheets. "I came straight back here after lunch. Why? What's going on?"

The two guards stopped what they were doing and looked at Alice, narrowing their eyes. Alice peered back, hitting them with her most innocent expression. They had nothing on her. All she had to do was ride this out.

"What's Ella got to do with anything?" Alice asked. Linda looked at the floor. "She's been attacked. Left for dead." She kicked her heel on the dusty tiles. "Did you see anything? Were you involved?"

Alice sat up and gasped. "Oh my God. I didn't see anything. Weren't you around? Or you, ma'am?"

The guards looked at each other. Looked sheepish. "There was a problem with the changeover. We were short-staffed." Sarah-Jane snapped. Then, more adamant. "We can't be everywhere at once."

Alice frowned, laying it on thick. "I understand. Still curious what you want from me though? As I say, I came back here straight after lunch."

"The Governor wants to see you," Linda said. "You have to come with us."

Alice tensed. If they searched her room while she was gone, they'd find all the evidence they needed. Luckily for her, Linda and Sarah-Jane were too preoccupied in saving their own necks to worry about who did what to whom. For the entire journey to the Governor's office they whispered to each other in a panicked manner. Getting their story straight. Down the next corridor two ambulance crew ran past and Alice felt the weight of something heavy on her soul. But it was the memory of Karen's murder, she realised. There was no guilt here.

They got to Jabba's office a few minutes later and Linda rapped loudly on the door. Alice could hear movement in the room. Furniture. Papers shuffling. Then a loud, austere voice.

"Enter."

Alice looked at Linda, who beckoned her into the room. "We'll wait here to escort you back," she told her. "The whole place is on lockdown."

Alice eased open the door and stepped inside.

"Close the door and sit down," Jabba snapped. She was reading something on her desk and didn't look up.

Alice did as she was told and settled into the hard chair, resting her forearms on the armrest. She took a deep breath. The way Jacqueline had shown her. A way to calm herself if she got too worked up. Jacqueline said it was a useful tool for someone like Alice, who was prone to bursts of heightened energy. Right now that energy was soaring through her and she knew it could take her over if she wasn't careful. She noticed a large jade paperweight on Jabba's desk, shaped like an egg. It was in reaching distance. One swoop of her arm, one leap, and she'd be on her - caving Jabba's head in.

Alice closed her eyes. Took another deep breath. Held it in her chest. It was this sort of thing Jacqueline had been talking about. Compulsion. Brought on by Alice's chattering moods. She had to learn to harness them better, Jacqueline had said. Hone them so they could be an asset rather than a curse.

"You know why you're here?" Jabba asked, looking up at Alice.

Alice shook her head. "No, ma'am. I was listening to some music and they brought me here. I take it something has happened with Ella but as I say, I was in my room."

Jabba sat back in her chair and steepled her index fingers over her concave chest. "Ella has been attacked, Alice. Severely. They're taking her to hospital now, but it's touch and go they say. She's received terrible head injuries and lost an eye. Now, are you telling me, girl, you had nothing at all to do with this?"

Alice's eyes grew wide. "I certainly did not. What a terrible thing, ma'am. I do hope she's all right."

The Governor stared at her, the same way the guards had been doing. Alice smiled her sweetest smile back.

"The paramedics couldn't say at this stage," Jabba muttered. "They had trouble reviving her." She narrowed her eyes. Then the tongue came out, licking slowly around her thin lips as she considered her next move. Her trademark. Why the girls all called her, Jabba.

"Is there anything else, ma'am?" Alice asked. "Only I have laundry duty soon and then a session with Ange…Ms. Baran."

Jabba kept going with her long, pink tongue. She was pissed off, Alice could tell. But she had nothing but suspicion. Wasn't enough. Her mind drifted to her next therapy session. She wondered what Jacqueline would have to say about what she'd done. Wondered if she should tell her outright.

"Very well," Jabba said. "But I'll be watching you, girl. If you put a foot wrong, I'll know about it." She stood up and moved around the front of the desk, so she was inches away from Alice. She tugged at the loose skin under one elbow with a bony, liver-spotted hand. It was subtle and she stopped immediately, but Alice had seen it. A tell. She was nervous. The old witch.

The knowledge filled Alice with a euphoria she hadn't felt for some weeks. Months even. It wasn't so much the fact she'd seen through Jabba's hardened veneer, but more so that she was able to. Her heightened moods were working with her for once. Honed and targeted. Like Jacqueline had explained.

"Well, that's fine, ma'am," Alice replied, getting to her feet. She was a good few inches taller than Jabba and her body was strong and agile. She could crush her with the flick of her wrist. They both knew it. But that would be stupid and pointless. "Thank you for the talk." Alice hit her once more with the sweetest of smiles. "I promise you don't need to worry about me. I won't be putting a foot wrong in here. Now, is that all?"

Jabba scowled at her. "I decide when you're dismissed, girl."

Alice held her ground. The room melted around her. Nothing mattered. She felt invincible. The chatter in her head was loud, a swelling pressure across her synapses. For once it wasn't unpleasant. She held Jabba's eyes. Didn't blink.

"Linda," Jabba yelled, over Alice's shoulder. "Ms. Vandella is ready to go back to her room." She moved back around the desk and sat down as Linda eased open the door. She didn't look up again as Alice was led out of her office. And that, as far as Alice was concerned, spoke volumes. She'd won this one. Now she had to work on keeping her moods up and her energy aimed in the right direction.

FOURTEEN

ALICE STUFFED HER BLOOD-SPLATTERED CLOTHING INTO A pillowcase and smuggled the whole lot into the laundry. As planned. In fact, the whole mission had gone just the way she'd hoped. She closed the washer door and selected the hottest wash available before letting out a deep sigh of relief.

It was over.

For now at least.

Whether Big Ella survived the attack or not wasn't important. Alice had gotten revenge for Karen. She'd made that nasty cow pay for what she'd done. Best of all, no one could ever pin it on her. There was no proof. No evidence she was anywhere near Big Ella when she was attacked. She'd slipped away, silently. Like Jacqueline had told her to.

However, she did wonder whether lack of evidence would matter to some of the more officious and vindictive guards here at Crest Hill, Jabba included. They could still make her life a misery if they wanted. Yet, with the further complication of the guards messing up the changeover, the hope was the authorities would brush the whole thing under the carpet and never mention it again.

Word would get out, of course, that she'd done it. Rumours travelled fast in this place and the rest of the girls would know and fear her. Alice would gain a new-found status in the home. Not her main driver for what she'd done, but a welcome bonus all the same.

"Alice, come in. Make yourself comfortable." After lunch, it was Alice's first session of the week with Jacqueline. Her first session since she'd attacked Big Ella.

She shuffled into the brightly lit room and sat down on the chair opposite Jacqueline. The room smelled different from usual. Something more medicinal underneath the spicy incense that normally laced the air. Though Alice wondered if it was her noticing it more readily. Her senses were on fire these last few days. She was able to pick out precise sounds, notice specific smells. It was disorientating. She was suddenly privy to more information than she knew what to do with.

"Can I have a glass of water?" Alice asked as Jacqueline went through her usual routine - rummaging through her files for Alice's case notes.

"Of course, one second." She looked up. "How are you feeling today?"

A shrug. "Fine."

Jacqueline found Alice's file and sat down opposite her. She smiled and let out a calming sigh, meaning Alice should do the same. Grounding the session. She'd forgotten Alice's water.

"A lot seems to have happened since the last time I saw you.

It was terrible what happened, wasn't it?"

"Yeah, awful," Alice said. "Crazy times."

"Do you perhaps want to talk about what happened to Ella?"

Alice frowned. "Why would I want to do that?"

"She was attacked. Rather brutally I heard. Lost an eye. It seems she might have permanent brain damage." She blew her cheeks out, but it was a clichéd expression. Her playing up to the role of concerned adult.

Alice didn't blink. She could read Jacqueline better now. This was a test.

"People are saying it looked like some sort of revenge attack," she continued. "What do you think?"

Alice considered the question. Pretended to, at least. "I think it was awful what happened," she said. "I abhor violence and I hope Ella gets better as soon as possible. That poor girl."

Jacqueline stared at her for a few seconds, letting a slight smile appear at the corners of her mouth. "So you had nothing to do with it?"

Alice opened her mouth in shocked horror. "Absolutely not. I was in my room when it happened. I can appreciate people might have thought I had something to do with it, after the rumours about Big Ella killing Karen. But as Linda and Sarah-Jane saw - I was on my bed, with not a spot of blood on me." She smiled at Jacqueline. She was enjoying this now. This dance. Her sparring with the therapist. "I mean, if I had been involved, I'd have been covered in it, no?" She made no disguise of the delight in her voice.

Jacqueline narrowed her eyes, serious now. "Good. Well done."

Alice sat forward. "Can I have that glass of water now, please?"

"Yes, of course." Jacqueline got up and moved around to the far side of the room where a jug of water and four glasses were standing on a carved, Moroccan-style table. She moved cat-like, stealthily. A far cry from the ditzy woman she often portrayed. Alice wondered which was the act. Wondered if either was for her benefit. These sessions with Jacqueline recently found Alice wondering a whole lot of things. She also couldn't help but stare at the therapist's lithe body as she poured out the water. Her slim, athletic legs in those tight black jeans. The curve of her breasts, stretching at the material of her blouse. A stirring tingled Alice's awareness, but she pushed it away. It was stupid. She liked boys.

"Why are you helping me?" Alice asked, surprising even herself.

Jacqueline turned and raised one eyebrow. "This is my job, Alice. I'm here to help all the girls with any underlying personal or psychological issues they might have." She brought the water over and placed it gently on the side table next to Alice. Jacqueline smelt good. Like exotic spices. She lingered there, her face inches from Alice's. "There you go - a nice glass of water." She sat back down.

Alice swallowed. "I don't mean the therapy," she said, speaking slowly, choosing her words. "All this – advice – about how to – conduct – myself in here. Why?"

Jacqueline sat back in her chair and tilted her head to one side. Her hair was thick and wavy, and her fringe had grown so it grazed the top of her eyes. Alice liked it. Her own hair was styled in a grown-out page boy cut. She hated it. Her mum had insisted she get it cut before she came inside.

"Let's just say I see something in you, Alice," Jacqueline whispered. "You remind me of myself when I was your age. I went through a similar situation as you. Sort of. Someone hurt my sister, not my mum. But the difference was I didn't do anything about it. I've always regretted that."

Alice nodded. "What about the other things you said? Strike silent. One at a time."

Jacqueline's expression dropped. "I don't want the system to destroy you, Alice. Like I've seen it do with so many girls. You've got potential. You're bright, funny, creative, attractive. You could be anything you want to be, but now is the time to stand up for yourself. Do you see? You're going to be in this home for the next few years at least. You're going to have to fight if you want to get out in one piece. Physically and mentally."

Alice snorted. "I'm not sure I've ever been in one piece mentally."

"No, well. Maybe that's what I like about you too."

"What? My biting sarcasm?"

"You don't take yourself too seriously, do you? But what I meant was you're a little bit broken. I recognise that in myself. I guess, with my therapist hat on I'm trying to help you so I can heal the young girl I used to be."

"You're helping me out of selfish reasons?"

"Bloody hell, Alice. Isn't everyone, if they're honest about it?"

Alice thought about it. "I guess we both benefit." Jacqueline leaned forward, speaking low and quick.

"As I said before, I can't have you disclosing to me what

you've done. But I can help you prepare for what you do. I can help you understand who you are. Help you to better cope with your personality traits – your moods. Teach you how to use what you've got a lot better."

She sat back, speaking in her usual volume and tone. "You need to survive, but you need to be clever about it as well. That's what we'll work on. Now, do you have any questions? Anything you want to add?"

Alice thought about it a moment. "That sounds good. Thank you. I appreciate you helping me."

Jacqueline smiled. "I think we can make a successful and confident person out of you, yet. Alice Vandella."

II

With the bottle gripped tightly in her fist, Alice launched herself forward. The man was much taller than her and strong with it, but he was also strung out on whatever substances had urged him on in this bloody assault.

And he didn't have her rage inside of him.

He swung a big ham-fist her way, but he was slow and underestimated her.

That was his second mistake.

She ducked under his arm and elbowed him in the ribs, forcing him back against the breakfast bar. He yelled out as his spine jammed into the countertop, and she followed up with a punishing knee to the groin. Another yell and he stumbled forward, cupping himself in case of further attack, leaving his face and neck exposed.

That was his fatal mistake.

A noise like a million chattering voices screamed across her consciousness. She raised the broken bottle and lunged forward, goring the sharp shards into the man's exposed throat. She ground the broken glass in deep, blood spurting from the wound and hitting her in the face with a force that shook her. It was warm. Thick. Plenty of it. The man cried out in pain as his eyes bulged out of their sockets.

Alice had taken enough interest in biology class to know she'd severed the Carotid artery, and she'd watched enough films to know he was already dead. But still he came for her, lunging forward, desperate hands clawing for purchase as he grabbed the material of her school shirt.

Not a chance.

Five years of Judo training paid off as she swept his legs from under him and he crashed onto the kitchen floor, the impact knocking most of the air out of him. He reached out and grabbed hold of her mum's leg, dragging her towards him in an attempt to pull himself upright.

No.

Wasn't going to happen.

She stamped down on his groin before straddling his torso and stabbing the bottle edge deep into the fleshy area underneath his chin. The chattering voices in her head grew in intensity as she continued her frenzied attack, stabbing and slashing and goring as the man screamed in pain beneath her. He grabbed at her. Lifted his hips to try and get her off him.

But it was no use.

He'd already lost a lot of blood and was weak, unable to defend himself.

She kept going, slashing and cutting wildly with the broken bottle as thick warm crimson splattered in her eyes and face.

Then, as if a switch had been turned off, she stopped and got to her feet. She gazed down at the mess of blood and flesh that was once Oscar Duke, her mother's abuser.

"You bastard," she whispered as the wine bottle slid from her fingers. She watched as it rolled away from her and came to a stop next *to the fridge.*

Then she flopped onto her mother's chest and burst into tears.

"Come right in, make yourself at home," Jacqueline said as Alice barged into the room without knocking.

She moved to her usual chair and sat down. "Do you have anything to drink?"

"Water. Like always."

Alice grinned. "Anything stronger."

Jacqueline moved from her desk and sat down in the chair opposite. She eyed Alice sternly. "That was a one-off. You know that."

"Oh, bloody hell, Jacqueline, calm down." She flicked her thick hair back over her shoulder. "I enjoyed it though, never had neat whisky before. Could get used to it."

Jacqueline frowned. "Your voice sounds different."

Alice stopped, her momentum faltering. She looked at her hands. "All right. Get over it."

The truth was she had been practicing her speaking voice recently - copying Jacqueline's intonation and inflection. It would do her well for when she got out of here. Plus, she liked disappearing behind a new persona. Like Bowie. It felt liberating.

"It's fine. You want to better yourself," Jacqueline told her. "I understand."

"I'm trying to speak proper," Alice told her. "Nothing wrong with that is there?"

"You're trying to speak properly," Jacqueline corrected. "And no. There's absolutely nothing wrong with that at all. Your hair looks good by the way. Nice fringe."

"Thanks."

"It's like mine."

Another shrug. "Whatever. Fancied a change is all."

The therapist smiled. "What do you want to talk about today?"

Alice had been seeing Jacqueline for over two years by this stage and the ninety minutes spent with her twice a month continued to be a much-needed tonic. Life at Crest Hill was now on an even keel, but she still had the chaotic intensity of her mind to deal with.

"Do you want to talk about he bats?" Jacqueline asked.

"In what way?"

"Last time it felt to me like we were getting a real handle on your condition. This metaphor you came up with 'the bats' as a way of explaining your manic episodes, I felt it was a useful tool. A way of distancing who you are from what's happening inside of you."

Alice rolled her head around her shoulders. "Yeah. I mean – yes - I think so. It feels correct. It certainly feels like there's a lot of bats fluttering about inside of me."

"Do you feel like you're able to cope with those feelings better by disengaging with them in this way?" Jacqueline asked.

Alice nodded. "It makes me feel more powerful. And as long as I channel these feelings, they don't have to crush me, or stop me doing anything."

Jacqueline beamed. "Good to hear, Alice. You've made so much progress. I'm proud of you." She raised one eyebrow. "You're Queen Bee of the place now, I hear."

Alice smiled. "What do you mean?"

"You know what I mean. You've got free run of the

place. Well respected by everyone," she paused. "Or well feared, maybe."

"Is there a difference?"

Jacqueline scoffed. "Perhaps not. But you're enjoying your new standing."

Alice got up and walked over to the window. The sky outside was a soft blue. A single starling flew across the scene. "You made me like this," she said.

"Is that what you think?"

"It's what I know. You helped me to understand how to go about things properly. If you hadn't, I'd probably be in real prison by now. Or dead."

Alice stared out the window. She hadn't been outside in days. Once compulsory, the guards now let Alice choose how she wanted to use her yard time. She had, however, been making good use of the new gymnasium, working out for an hour or more every day for the last three months. And it showed. She stretched her arms in front of the window and arched her back, making her sweatshirt ride up. She was annoyed at herself for doing it, but a part of her wanted Jacqueline to notice.

"You're looking very athletic these days. Exercise doing you good?"

Alice smiled out the window. "It's fun. I used to be pretty fit so it's good to get back into it. Useful. You know." She turned back around. "In case anyone is planning on dethroning the Queen."

"I see," Jacqueline said, as Alice returned to her seat. "Have you thought about what you might do when you get out of Crest Hill?"

Alice sat back. "What do girls usually do?"

"Most re-offend," Jacqueline said. "It's a pattern. This is why I've always instilled in you – don't be another statisitic. You're far too bright to fall into petty crime and end up in jail, Alice. You hear me?"

"What do you suggest?" Alice asked. "Get an office job? Receptionist? Little Dolly Bird behind a keyboard?"

"Don't be daft. You've got a lot going for you. You've such an interesting brain. Plus, you've got your - insatiable killer instinct - shall we say. You'd do well in the police or the army."

Alice screwed her nose up. "The police? You serious?"

"All I'm saying is - don't waste your talents. You'll be out of here in three years. You'll be twenty-one. The world at your feet. Hell, you could even become a hired killer if you wanted."

Alice frowned. "Excuse me?"

Jacqueline brushed it off. "A joke. But you've got the right skill set. The right type of personality. Which is why I think the military or the police would be a great option."

The rest of the session passed by in a blur. Alice was only half-listening, only half-engaged as Jacqueline turned the talk to her condition. There was a label now for it. Bipolar Disorder, Dr Richards had called it. Though Alice was a special case, she'd said. Something along those lines, she hadn't been paying much attention. It didn't matter to Alice what they called her condition, only how she learned to manage it. And she was learning. Exercise helped, keeping a food diary too. They said her condition might even be an asset if she could harness it the right way. That was the hope at least.

"I'll see you in a few weeks," Jacqueline was saying,

leaning forward and putting a hand on Alice's knee. "Are you okay?"

"Sorry. Yeah. Yes. I'm good." Good, but a little dazed. "I was thinking about what you said before. About what to do next."

"Well do give it some more thought," Jacqueline said, getting to her feet. She placed a hand on Alice's lower back and gently guided her to the door. "You're a very interesting girl, Alice Vandella. Use your powers for good, won't you?" Then as they got to the door, she lowered her voice and winked. "Or if you can't use them for good, make sure you use them for something that gives you a good life." Then like before, she brightened up. As if a different person was speaking. "So have a good couple of weeks. Stay out of trouble and I'll see you soon."

Alice stood outside the office as the door closed behind her. She liked Jacqueline. Really liked her. There were even times recently when Alice wondered if she might even be in love with her. But she certainly was confusing.

The clock above Jacqueline's door read half-past one. Visiting time was an hour away and Alice's mum was on the list. The thought hit her with the usual feelings of elation and dread. The way it was now. She decided to head back to her room and rest for a while. Jacqueline's speech had rattled her, and she needed a straight head before she met with Louisa.

These days Alice didn't get escorted around the building by the guards. No-one did. Unless they were high-risk. To themselves or others. Jabba had resigned at the start of the year and the new governor - Diane Charles – had brought with her a more modern and relaxed approach. She believed strong boundaries were important for the girls, but just as vital was creating a culture of mutual respect and trust. So gone was the oppressive, prison-like atmosphere. The guards were encouraged to call the girls by their first names, and nothing was off-limits. Within reason. Meaning the girls were free to roam around as they pleased. They could watch as much TV as they wanted and the only real stipulations were lights out at half-ten and only thirty girls to the TV room or library at any one time. It had worked too, so far. Cases of suicide and violent attacks had both dropped considerably since Diane had arrived. Though Alice knew that was as much down to her own influence. If you asked any of the girls in Crest Hill these days they'd tell you, Alice Vandella made the rules.

And she was not someone to mess with.

FIFTEEN

"THERE SHE IS - MY LITTLE ANGEL."

Alice heard her mum's voice the second she stepped into the visitor's block but kept her head down, didn't let on. Louisa stood, waving.

"Alice? Alice over here."

"Sit down, please," Alice muttered to herself.

She'd asked her mum many times to wear conservative clothing when visiting, but she never did. Today she wore an orange dress made from t-shirt material. It was skin-tight and far too short. Worse still, she'd put on weight and the dress was unforgiving. Her skin was pale, and the heavy mascara did little to hide the dark circles under her eyes.

Alice sat opposite her and smiled. "Hi Mum," she said. "How are you?"

"I'm all right. Like always. But never mind me. How are you, Sweetie?"

Alice screwed her nose up. "Same as always, you know."

An awkward, but typical, silence fell between them.

Louisa fiddled with a gold bangle on her wrist. "You

look well," she said."

"There's a new gym block, so I've been going there. Weights and stuff. Getting into it again."

Her mum smiled and Alice saw her teeth looked yellow. Back on the cigarettes. "Are you looking after yourself?"

"Yes. I am. It's been difficult for me these last few months since Steve left. But I keep on going. You have to, don't you?"

Alice sneered. Steve. One of her mum's old punters. An ugly fat slob from what Alice remembered. But he had cash and a steady job so once Louisa gave up the game, she'd taken him in. Let him provide for her. In turn, he got a free bunk-up and someone to cook for him. It was a decent enough arrangement, Alice had thought, especially while she was inside. That was until Steve had his head turned by the sixteen-year-old barmaid at his local pub and packed his bags. Now Louisa had no one.

"You deserved better than him anyway," Alice told her. "Did I?" She looked away, but Alice had already clocked

the deep sadness in her eyes. It was always there, only now was she couldn't mask it so well. Or she didn't try to.

"I'll be out of here in a few years," Alice told her. "Maybe less. Jacqueline says if I keep up my sessions with her – and my studies – then she'll put in a good word for me with the board. Maybe get me early release as a reformed character."

"Well, you are, aren't you?" Louisa sat upright and stuck her sizeable breasts forward in defiance. "You never did anything wrong apart from one time. And we all know you were only looking out for me. My little hero you are. My little Acid Vanilla."

"Mum. Don't." Alice scowled and glanced around the room. Two tables away, Slow Ella – so-called now after the contrecoup injuries she received - looked over and waved. With her eyepatch and limp, she was no longer any threat. Just a little annoying. "I told you, please. Don't ever call me that."

Her mum laughed. "Aw come off it. That's what you used to call yourself, Acid Vanilla. You were such a funny little thing. You thought you were saying your name properly, you just got it mixed up. We all thought it was the cutest thing."

"Stop it. It's stupid." Alice shook her head. "I never want to hear that name again. I was a silly little kid."

"You're still my silly little kid, always will be."

"Well, I'm not. I'm eighteen, Mum."

Louisa's face dropped. She went white. "Eighteen. Oh my god? I'm so sorry Al."

"What do you mean?"

"I forgot your birthday. You're eighteenth."

Alice leaned back in her chair and folded her arms. She considered her mum's expression. Was she trying to be funny?

"You didn't forget," she told her. "You were here. On the day. You brought me cake. Remember?"

Louisa stared at Alice. Though in truth, she was staring through her. Her eyes widened, teeming with confusion - but it was more than that – she was scared.

Then she smiled.

"Yes. Of course I remember. I'm only being daft. Eighteen. An adult. Where did the time go?"

A frown furrowed Alice's brow. "Yeah. Weird."

"So anyway, you say you might be getting out sooner rather than later? That is good news."

Alice sniffed. "They want me to consider what I'll do when I get out. Jobs and stuff. There's a new program being set up to help girls like me get into work."

"Wonderful."

The two women exchanged smiles, nervous glances. A shared realisation that life would be changing soon enough.

Prior to Jacqueline bringing up the matter, Alice hadn't given too much thought to what she'd do when free. She'd been enjoying her new Queen Bee status too much. Living day-to-day. Now all at once the future was rushing to meet her and she wasn't ready for it. Not one bit. Alice wondered if this is what people meant when they talked about being institutionalised.

When visiting time ended Alice hugged her mum close and told her she'd see her soon, to take care of herself. As she was heading back to her room, she bumped into one of the new girls, Sadie.

"That your mum, is it?" Sadie asked as they pushed through the double doors and made their way into the corridor towards Alice's block.

Alice didn't look at her. "Yes, that's my mum. What of it?"

"She looks young. Looks like you. Reckon that's what you'll turn out like?"

Alice paused. Turned to face her. She was mixed race and had a naturally athletic body. Broad shoulders and long limbs. She looked like she could do some damage if she put her mind to it.

"How do you mean?" Alice asked.

Sadie smirked and leaned forward. "A slag," she rasped. "I heard all about her. About what you did. You think you're proper hard don't you, Vandella. Well, guess what? So am I."

"Is that so?" Alice said, moving closer to her. "If you've heard about me, you know what I can do." Her voice went low. As sinister as it got. "Now apologise, or I will fucking crucify you."

Sadie's eyes widened. "Come on then, bitch. Let's go." She leaned forward, their faces only centimetres apart. "Alice? What's going on?" The two girls stepped back as

Jacqueline appeared around the corner. She came up to them. "Well? Should you be here - either of you?"

The girls looked down. Said, "No ma'am."

"Right then. And you, what's your name? Are you new?"

Sadie sniffed. Her head bowed. "Sadie Jones. I arrived two weeks ago."

Jacqueline placed her hand under Sadie's chin and lifted her head.

"I suppose you want to make a name for yourself, do you?" She leaned in close, whispering. "I'm guessing you know Alice is Head Girl around here, and you want the spot. But it doesn't work like that." She placed her other hand on Sadie's shoulder. Waited until she looked her in the eyes. "You're lucky I split this up when I did. She'd have killed you. So, you have a good think, girl, about what you do next in here. Because it's not only Alice that will be down on you if you come for her. Do you understand what I'm saying?"

Sadie stared up at Jacqueline, as though not quite

comprehending what she was hearing. Alice swallowed. That made two of them.

"Do you understand?" Jacqueline asked, speaking slowly as if to a child. "You come at Alice again, your life won't be worth living." Sadie nodded and Jacqueline brightened once more. "Good. Now get to your room and we won't hear any more about this."

Alice and Jacqueline watched in silence as Sadie shuffled away.

Alice turned to Jacqueline. "Thank you. But why?"

Jacqueline shook her head. "We don't need to discuss this. But let me reiterate to you, Alice: Be careful. Don't get caught. You're developing a valuable set of skills, and a personality to match. But you need to keep on guard with your emotions. That chaos we talked about – sharpen it, control it. Make those bats work for you. Not against you."

Alice's mouth hung open. "I get that. But what I don't understand is - why are you doing this? Helping me? This isn't what therapists do."

Jacqueline looked over her shoulder, then back at Alice. "I told you, I see a lot of myself in you. But yes – maybe I do have a vested interest in your development. I can't say too much. But expect a visit in the next few weeks. From someone who can help you."

Alice was about to ask who, but Jacqueline was already walking away.

She called back, "Now get to your room and stay out of trouble. You hear me, Alice Vandella?" She winked knowingly, then disappeared through the double doors that led to the staff quarters.

SIXTEEN

Alice was lying on her bed a week later when there was a loud knock on the door. "Vande...Alice?" It was Linda's voice.

Alice slid off the bed and opened the door. "What's going on."

"You've got a visitor."

Alice frowned. "No. My mum's not due until next week."

"Not your mum," Linda mumbled. "Your uncle. He said you arranged it a few months ago."

Alice was about to tell Linda she didn't have an uncle, not one she knew about anyway, but something stopped her.

"Fine," she said. "I'll come see him."

Linda leaned against the doorframe. "I've been told to escort you. Just in case."

Alice pulled her sweater on. "In case what?"

"Don't know. What they told me."

Alice pondered this, then gestured for Linda to lead the way. They walked in silence to the visitor's block.

"In the far corner," Linda whispered, pointing over to where a large man was sitting, gazing out the window. "Your uncle."

Alice looked at Linda, looked back at the man. "Great, thanks."

She made her way slowly over to the table watching the man as she did. He had huge hands clasped in front of him on the table. Each finger held a heavy silver ring. Some were jewelled, some skull-shaped, some medallion. He saw Alice as she approached and stood to meet her. He was tall as well as broad, well over six feet. He wore a lime green polo-necked jumper and a long tan leather coat with a fur collar. He smiled as Alice got close, exposing two gold canines.

"Alice, lovely to see you," he growled. "Please sit."

His accent was strange - cockney but with an affected tone. As though attempting to better himself. It warmed him to Alice as she sat down.

"Who are you?" she asked.

The man frowned and spread his arms. "I'm your uncle."

Alice leaned forward, speaking softly. "I don't have an uncle. What's going on?"

The man closed his eyes and sighed. Then he smiled. "All right let's start again. Let me introduce myself properly, my name is Beowulf Caesar." He held out his hand.

Alice leaned back and smirked. "Beowulf Caesar? Are you fucking kidding me? That's not your real name."

He narrowed his eyes. "I didn't say it was my real name. But it's the only name I go by these days."

Alice nodded in quick agreement. It was the man's tone.

The way his face dropped from jollity to threatening solemnity. He unnerved her.

"What do you want?" she asked. "Why are you pretending to be my uncle?"

Beowulf Caesar folded his arms and looked Alice dead in the eye. His eyes were intense with malice creeping in at the corners.

"Because I've heard a lot about you, Alice Vandella. About what you did, and about how you're conducting yourself in here. Your case was of interest to me the moment I read about it. You've got something special. I know it. Something I want."

Alice frowned. "Well tough luck. I'm not into that."

He waved her down. "Oh, fuck off. Look at me. I don't do soft and moist. I prefer my sexual partners a tad more – tumescent – shall we say?"

Alice watched him. If she had to guess she'd say he was in his early forties. Although he had good skin. His whole look was menacing but well-groomed. It made sense now.

"What do you want from me?"

"I want you to work for me. With me. In a new organisation I'm setting up. One that will radicalise and disrupt the whole industry."

Alice chewed her lip. "What industry?"

Caesar held up his hands. "All in good time. But it's a job for life if you want it. In fact, I insist on it. I've been scouting the land - the world, even - looking for the right people for what I want to create. And you, my dear, fit the bill perfectly. They say you're super intelligent and have a creative flair, as well as a logical mindset. They say you're strong, athletic, wily. And I can see you are. But most importantly - they say you've got killer instinct. That's what I need."

"Killer instinct?" Alice's mind raced to what Jacqueline had said in their last session.

Caesar grinned. "My dream is an elite service for people who need a problem removing." His face lit up as he whispered. "I'm talking about an assassin network, Alice. Killing people for money. Lots of money. A shit-load."

He sat back and stared at Alice. But she gave nothing away. This despite her heart pounding heavily in her chest and an immense pressure forming in her head. The bats were screaming across her consciousness. Telling her, this was what she'd been waiting for. What she'd been preparing for.

"And you want me to – do that – for you?" Alice asked. "With me. Alongside me. I'm assembling a crack team.

The best of the best. People who are ready to start their lives afresh. From year zero. I hear you fit both of those criteria, no?"

Alice thought of her mum. "Maybe," is all she said.

"As a sweetener Alice, and to prove I'm serious – I'll get you out of this dump. Within the next few months. Ensure your remaining time goes by a whole lot easier too."

The skin on Alice's arms tingled. This whole exchange felt super-real. Like she was dreaming. "How? I've got another three years, at least."

Caesar closed his eyes. "You don't have to worry about the hows, my dear. But enough for today." He got to his feet. "Think about my offer. A new life. Full of opportunity. More money than you've ever seen. I'll be back in one week for your answer."

Alice stood. "I don't think I can..." she started, but Caesar held up his hand.

"Think about it this week. Then we'll talk." He leaned forward. "Picture it, Alice. Being part of a new, elite, organisation. An exclusive service that will bring us riches beyond our wildest dreams. You've got what it takes, Alice. I can see that. Consider my offer. Won't you?"

With that, he moved around the table and rested a large hand on Alice's shoulder. He held it there for a moment, then walked off, leaving Alice to wonder what the hell had just happened.

SEVENTEEN

ALICE DIDN'T SLEEP A WINK THAT NIGHT, OR THE NEXT night. Her mind was a whirlwind of opposing thoughts and ideas. Not to mention a whole heap of unanswerable questions and niggling worries. When she wasn't tossing and turning in bed, she spent her time in the gym, on the treadmill - an attempt to sweat out the chattering pressure and rushes of intense mania.

Every cell in her body burned with a concentrated vigour, and she couldn't be certain whether it felt good or not. Life was a fine line for Alice these days. Good and evil. Wellness and depression. Madness and sanity. She lived in a constant state of turmoil, straddling these twin elements of her personality.

On the third day after Caesar's visit, she found herself knocking on Jacqueline's door. She didn't have a session until a week Tuesday, but she needed to talk. Needed to get whatever was inside of her out, before it ate her alive.

"Alice? This is a surprise." There was something about

the way Jacqueline spoke that troubled Alice. Like she was expecting the visit. "Please, come in."

Alice moved over to her usual chair but didn't sit. There was a bookcase along the side wall. She absent-mindedly selected a leather-bound tome and read the title, *Alice Through the Looking Glass.*

Jesus.

She replaced it and sat down as Jacqueline closed the door. "What can I do for you?" she asked. "You got something on your mind?"

Alice blew out her cheeks. "Did you know he was coming to see me?"

Jacqueline looked puzzled. "Did I know who was coming to see you?"

Alice slumped onto her usual chair and pulled her knees up, hugging them to her.

"What is it, Alice? You seem troubled."

"I am."

"Okay. Talk to me."

Alice looked up at the ceiling. "I don't know what to do. I thought everything was getting back to normal this last year. Well, not normal. But easier. Simpler. Then this fucking guy comes to visit, says he's my uncle, says he can get me out of here. It's all so weird. And then there's this thing with my mum. Shit. I don't know what to do." She gasped. She'd been speaking fast, without a breath.

Jacqueline sat opposite her and smiled in that way she often did. Half-way between compassion and condescension.

"I'm sorry," she said. "I'm not following. Why don't you

take a moment, compose yourself, and start at the beginning? Who is this man who came to visit?"

It seemed like a genuine question. Jacqueline's face gave nothing away.

"He calls himself Beowulf Caesar," Alice said. "He knew all about me. Why I'm in here. Said he knew about what I'd done inside - Big Ella. Shit, sorry."

She looked away. The unwritten rule still stood. Alice wasn't to talk about her actions to Jacqueline. Best for them both.

Jacqueline twisted her mouth to one side. "Beowulf Caesar? That's a name and a half, isn't it?"

"It's not his real name."

"No shit."

Jacqueline laughed and Alice did too. The ice was broken. Alice released her knees and made herself more comfortable on the chair.

"He wants me to work for him. Says I'll make a lot of money. Says he can get me out of here if I agree."

"I see. What would you be doing?"

Alice sniffed back. "Killing people." She laughed as she said it, as though it was the most ridiculous thing she'd ever said. It was.

But Jacqueline nodded, poker-faced. "Was he serious?"

"Seemed to be. Do you believe it? He said he's scouting the world, looking for people who fit his criteria. People with a killer instinct - who are happy to leave their past behind. People like me, I guess."

"And are you?" Jacqueline asked. "Happy to leave your past behind?"

Alice looked at the ceiling. "I want to, shit. But there's

my mum. I'm worried about her. I think there's something wrong with her."

"What is it?"

"I'm not entirely sure. This last year she's getting more forgetful. She's always been ditzy, but this is different. I'll catch her looking at me at visiting times and it's the light has gone off in her eyes. I rang her yesterday and it took her a few seconds to remember my name. That's not good, is it?"

Jacqueline sighed. "It might be stress. It must be hard for her." She clocked Alice's expression and changed her tone. "It does also sound like early-onset dementia. Or Alzheimer's."

Alice nodded. "I've been reading up on it in the library. That's what I thought too. Bloody hell. What am I going to do? I can't look after her."

"You'll need money no doubt. For care. That sort of thing. If this Caesar is promising you lots of it. Well…'

Alice sat back. "Are you serious? You think I should take him up on his offer?"

Jacqueline was quiet for a long time. She closed her eyes, stretched her mouth, took some deep breaths. Then she stood up and slowly padded over to the window.

"I see a lot of young girls come through the system. Most of them are already too far gone before they get to me. They don't stand a chance. The best they can hope for is to meet some decent enough bloke, have a few kids - probably a few too many. Live out their lives in front of daytime TV." She turned around to meet Alice's gaze. "But then you walk into my office. You're clever, sharp, articulate, with a biting wit. You're also athletic, passionate, creative. Plus, when you aren't wearing all that eyeliner, you're very attractive. You've got everything going for you, Alice. But then there's this shadow side. This darkness, that you carry with you."

Alice's turn to sigh. "The bats?"

"Yes, the bats - and like we also explored – the flipside to your manic phases. What animal did you come up with in the end to describe it?"

Alice grinned. "A manatee."

"That's right, a bloody manatee. See? You're unlike anyone I've ever met, Alice. My point being - maybe normal life isn't right for someone like you. Does that make any sense?"

Alice nodded. It did. It was what she'd been thinking. Jacqueline went on, "I know it's absurd - and dangerous - that we're even having this conversation. But like I always say, you're a special case, Alice. If you were to accept this man's offer, you could help your mum. You could have a good life - on the outskirts of society."

"But I have to leave my past behind, that's what he said. Meaning no ties. How could I care for my mum?"

"There are ways, Alice. Homes. Places that will provide the best care. No one has to know you're doing it. Someone as bright as you - you'll find a way."

Alice joined Jacqueline at the window. "Did you know Caesar was coming to see me? Did you tell him about me?"

The two women stared out through the glass. Clouds peppered the blue expanse of sky and luscious leafy trees swayed gently in the breeze. It was the sort of spring day that made you feel good to be alive. If you weren't locked up in an institute.

"He contacted me last year." Jacqueline's voice was soft

but serious. "Told me what he told you. That he was looking for the best of the best. An elite task force."

"Who is he? How do you know him?"

Jacqueline didn't look at her. "He approached me after work. Outside my house. I was scared at first. Terrified, I'll be honest. But he's a charismatic sod, isn't he? Has a certain charm about him. At first I told him I couldn't help him, of course. Said I didn't know anyone who fitted his criteria. But as our sessions went on - after Big Ella was attacked and you started your fitness regime - I began to wonder."

Alice frowned. "Did he pay you?"

"I won't lie to you. Yes, he did. Quite a lot. For my silence obviously, and for any information. A finder's fee, as he put it."

"Jesus, Jacqueline. So, what? You're pimping me out? I thought you cared about me?"

The therapist snapped her eyes to meet Alice's. "I do care about you. That's why I decided to tell him about you. I'd wrestled with whether to for a long time but what he can offer you, Alice, it'll provide you with an amazing life. A life you won't have access to any other way." She walked away and sat down. "I know you want to work hard and get a job, and all that. But I don't think it's going to be easy for you. It never is. Even for someone as clever as you. The world is already against you, after being in here. You did kill someone, remember? Plus, what happened with Big Ella. Like I say - perhaps you aren't cut out for civilian life. This is your chance to be someone."

Alice snorted. "As long as I don't mind killing people. Have you heard yourself?"

Jacqueline closed her eyes. "I know. It's crazy. But the

way he explained it, the work you'd be doing would make the world a better place. You'd be getting rid of gangsters, drug dealers, corrupt government officials. What he's going to charge per job, Alice, when it costs so much you know the people involved usually deserve it."

"Wow," Alice said. "You've really made peace with this."

"It'll be the answer to all your problems. I believe that."

"But I could be out in two years. Three for certain. I want to go back to my trampolining, my judo. I could be a pro. Could make the Olympic team."

"Or you could struggle to get a job. Find yourself falling into petty crime, regardless. Get pregnant. Then what? Your life is over. Your potential's gone." Jacqueline stood up again, pacing. "You're a murderer, Alice. You stabbed a guy to death with a broken bottle. Practically decapitated him. Not to mention the fact you've ruled the roost around here for the past year with an iron fist. And what? You'll get out of here and get a job on the tills in Tesco? All I'm saying, Alice, is please think about it." Jacqueline glanced up at the clock. "I have a session in five minutes. I need to prepare."

She shuffled over to her desk at the far side of the room and busied herself with notepads and file notes. Alice watched her in silence. Then she stood up and without saying a word walked over to the door and let herself out.

EIGHTEEN

Caesar had told Alice he'd be back in a week for her answer. But a week rolled around and there was no sign of him. When two weeks passed - and then three and four - Alice wondered if she might have imagined the whole thing. If it wasn't for Jacqueline knowing the truth, she might have put it down to her condition - some sort of stress-induced delusion. But no. Beowulf Caesar was real. Or he had been at least. For whatever reason, he must have changed his mind about her.

In the weeks that followed Alice kept herself busy. She hit the gym hard, spent time in the library studying, working out what she might do when she was released. To think she'd even considered Caesar's proposal. What an idiot. She wasn't going to give her life up and work for some secret organisation. She was an eighteen-year-old girl from Dagenham, for heaven's sake. To even consider she might become an international assassin was ludicrous.

Alice had also given Jacqueline a wide berth since their last encounter. The more she'd pondered what they'd talked about, the more uneasy she felt about their relationship. She still had strong feelings for her therapist - she couldn't simply turn them off - but she'd seen something new underneath her façade of concern and therapeutic exchange. It wasn't nice.

Then, one Thursday afternoon - exactly two months after Caesar had first visited - Alice was called to the Governor's office. She was lying on her bed reading a library copy of Edgar Allen Poe's short stories when Linda put her head around the door.

"What? Now?" Alice asked her. "What does she want?"

"I don't know," Linda said. "I was told to come and get you. You've to bring all your stuff. You're probably moving rooms."

"All my stuff?" Alice looked around the room. "Like everything - everything? My books? CDs?"

Linda nodded. "That's what I was told. Here." She threw her a sack, made of rough plastic with handles on either side. "Pack it all in here. Be quick."

With a heavy frown knotting her brow, Alice slid off the bed and did as she was told. Not that it took her long. The girls weren't permitted many belongings in the institute – even Alice, whose status and reputation allowed her more leeway. She had books, CDs, make-up, a Bowie poster, that was about it. She left the poster where it was and stuffed the rest in the sack. She looked at Linda.

"All right. Let's go."

She followed on behind Linda through the winding corridors of the lower block. They passed the canteen, the library, the visiting hall. The only sound made was the squeak of Alice's pumps on the polished floor. "Here we are." They got to the Governor's office, and Linda stepped to one side. "She's expecting you, so straight in."

Alice went to respond but Linda was already striding off down the corridor. Alice turned back around and knocked on the large oak door.

"Come in, please."

Alice eased open the door to reveal the tall gangly figure of Diane Charles. She was perched on the edge of her desk reading a file. As Alice stepped into the room, she peered over the top of her half-moon glasses. She was only relatively young. Early thirties, Alice would have said, but the glasses and the tweed two-piece made her look so old. The hair bun didn't help.

"Ah, Alice Vandella," she said. "Please, come in."

She moved around the desk and sat down on the opposite side, gestured for Alice to sit.

"What's going on, ma'am?"

Diane looked nervous. More so than usual. She didn't look Alice in the eyes.

"How long have you been here now, Alice?"

She thought, "I'm eighteen as of last month. So over three years. Time flies when you're having fun." She laughed, but there was no humour to it.

Diane nodded stiffly. "Would you say your time here has been well spent? Do you feel - how can I put it - re-adjusted?"

Alice twisted a strand of hair around her finger. "Well, ma'am, it was only a freak occurrence why I was in here in the first instance. Before I did what I did, I was a good girl. Did well at school, involved in lots of extra-curricular activities." She smiled sweetly, giving it the full bit.

Diane's face relaxed. "Yes. Good. Very good. Well, Alice, I have good news for you. We – I – the authorities - we believe you've served your time and have been suitably rehabilitated. Thus, it makes no sense for someone with your potential to be delayed any longer. So, the decision has been made. You're to be released."

The words hung in the air. "What? Seriously?" Alice asked. "I wouldn't joke," Diane said. "When?"

"Today. Now. You won't need to go back to your room.

Do you have everything with you?"

Alice couldn't believe what she was hearing. She looked at the sack of belongings, then back to Diane. "Yeah, I think so."

Diane raised her chin, speaking to the room. She still wouldn't look Alice in the eyes. "Very well, I'll have the guard escort you to the holding unit and we'll contact your next of kin. You can either wait there for them to collect you or, seeing as you're eighteen we can escort you to the train station and put you on a train home."

Alice thought about it. "Can I say goodbye to people?"

"No, I'm sorry."

"What about Jacqueline, my therapist? She's been such a help."

"Fine. But quickly. I'll have Linda take you there then straight for an exit interview. It won't take long." She perused her notes a second. "In the meantime, I'll contact your mother and give her the news. She's the only person on your contact list, correct?"

"Yep, just me and her," Alice said.

Her mind swam with questions and possibilities as Linda led her to Jacqueline's office. She was being released. Today.

Three years early. It was a dream come true. So why did she have this ominous creeping sensation in her guts?

"Come in," Jacqueline sang as Alice knocked. Alice glanced at Linda, who gave her a curt nod.

"Five minutes," Alice told her. She went in and closed the door.

Jacqueline was sitting at her desk reading a magazine. She looked up as Alice entered and smiled. "I was hoping to see you today."

"Have you heard about what's going on?"

She looked over Alice's shoulder, making sure the door was shut. "I've heard. Yes. I'm happy for you."

"Are you?"

"Of course I am."

"Did you have something to do with it?"

Jacqueline didn't answer, she stood and moved over to Alice. She was dressed all in black. Black jeans, black shirt. Behind her on a coat stand hung a black leather jacket. Alice couldn't help but feel in awe of Jacqueline. Even after all this time. She came right up to her, their breasts almost touching. "Whatever happens next, Alice," she whispered. "I want you to remember, you can handle it. Follow your instincts. Always. They know what to do. Listen to them." Their proximity and Jacqueline's hushed voice sent ripples of electricity down Alice's neck. "You're a special person, Alice Vandella. You can do anything you want with your life. Choose well."

Alice looked into Jacqueline's face. Up close she was even prettier. Her eyes were cat-like. Sexy, but brutal.

"Thank you," Alice whispered. "I'm going to miss you."

"And I'll miss you too."

Their lips were inches apart. Alice closed her eyes as Jacqueline's hot breath brushed her against her cheek. She moved closer and opened her mouth. Waited. Then she felt a hand on her shoulder.

"You better get going."

Alice opened her eyes to see Jacqueline holding her at arm's length.

"Oh? Yes. Sure," she stammered. "I best had."

She sighed. But this was good news. She was getting out. Getting her life back on track. Her plan now was simple: go straight, get a job, look after her mum. She'd be a good daughter. A good citizen. She was healthy, intelligent, she could do anything she wanted.

Now if she could only work out what that was, she'd be fine.

NINETEEN

A BITING BREEZE SWIRLED AROUND ALICE'S HEAD AS SHE stepped through the main gates of Crest Hill and heard the large metal lock clink shut behind her.

Freedom.

It felt good. But also, incredibly strange. Diane had told Alice her mum would pick her up from the main gate and she was to wait for her. But she was late - as usual - and Alice wanted to get as far away from Crest Hill as possible. She looked both ways down the long straight road which ran past the front of the large building. There was no sign of any cars, but whichever dirty old sod was driving Louisa today, they'd be coming from London. Alice set off walking. She'd meet up with them along the way somewhere.

Despite the confusion fogging her head and the uncertainty regarding her future, she had a certain spring in her step. She was outside. In the fresh air. A free girl. A free woman. Eighteen now. She could do this. She was strong, powerful, invincible.

She jumped as a car horn beeped loudly behind her.

There was no pavement on this part of the road so she moved onto the worn grassy area so it could pass. But it didn't. It stayed behind her, creeping along, matching her pace. She tensed, assuming it to be a group of young men, trying to get her attention. She kept on walking. Didn't turn around. If her assumptions were correct, they'd be hooting and jeering at her the second she did. Even as an awkward fifteen-year-old goth, Alice had gotten a lot of unwanted attention from local boys in souped-up Fiats. Now as a young woman she only expected it more. Not something she was happy about.

The car beeped its horn again. Alice spun around. "Oh, piss off will y…'

But it wasn't testosterone-fuelled boys, and it certainly wasn't some boy-racer mobile. Instead, Alice gazed down at a large, jet-black BMW. It was so heavily polished she could see her reflection clear in the bonnet. Like a mirror. Behind the wheel was Beowulf Caesar. He grinned and beckoned her over

Alice gripped her sack of belongings to her as Caesar wound down the passenger window. He leaned over and smiled, exposing those gold wolf teeth.

"What are you doing here?" Alice said. "I thought you'd changed your mind?"

Caesar smirked. "Not my mind. My approach. I thought it might help you in your decision if I showed you what I can do for you."

"How do you mean?"

"Get in and I'll explain?"

Alice looked down the road. "I can't. My ride is on its way."

"This is your ride. No one else is coming."

Alice frowned. "What do you mean? The Governor, she said…'

"The Governor says what I tell her," Caesar growled. "Now sling your bag in the back and get in."

Alice halted a moment, then did as instructed. After slamming the back door shut, she climbed into the front seat beside Caesar.

"Good girl." He slipped a pair of oversized sunglasses on his face, shoved the stick in first, and pulled away.

It was a two-hour drive back to London. Alice sat back and made herself comfortable. She didn't know what to say so she said nothing. Enjoyed the journey as best she could. Caesar's car was big. The engine powerful, but soft. It felt to Alice like she was rocketing along on a steel cloud - a new experience for her. Andy Jenkins, the first boy she'd been with had had a car, but it was a noisy old banger, and you felt every pothole. Alice remembered the back seat - where she'd lost her virginity - had milkshake stains all over it and smelt of stale weed smoke. Caesar's car smelt like strawberries and the seats were made of soft, cream leather. The dashboard was made of polished resin.

They'd been driving for twenty minutes and had joined the M20 motorway when Caesar spoke again. "I take it you're over the moon to be out of that rotten place.

Alice scoffed. "Yes. Of course. It feels weird though - to be out." A pause. She watched out the window as trees turned into small bungalows, turned into factories and high-rises. "Like it's not real."

"Well, it's real all right." "But how?"

"I greased a few palms, shall we say. Believe me Alice,

there's not much people *won't* do when you're waving a stinking great wad of money under their nose."

"Where are we going?"

Caesar smiled. "I'm taking you home. You've got a lot to sort out."

Out the window, Alice began to recognise the area. The outskirts of East London. A few minutes later they passed the new Bluewater shopping centre. Alice had been planning on visiting before Oscar Duke came into her life. Another thirty minutes or so and she'd be home.

"Sort out what?" she asked. "When you didn't come back, I assumed you didn't want me to work for you any longer. I decided it was for the best. I'm going to get a job."

"Oh, come on now," Caesar barked. "Doing what?"

"I don't know. In a shop, at first. But I'm clever, I could do well in life. I've got a lot going for me."

"Modest too, hey?" Caesar laughed. "Be realistic though, Alice. Do you think people are going to give you a chance, after what you did? You murdered a man, Alice. All right, you could say it was self-defence, but the extent of it. I mean, fucking hell, you're a vicious one when you want to be, kid."

Alice kept her gaze out the window. Caesar leaned over and grabbed her thigh. Made her jump.

"What I'm saying is, I love your attitude. Why I want you to work for me. That vicious streak, coupled with your other qualities. Mwah." He kissed his fingers, like a chef tasting something delicious. "Work for me and you could make in one month - hell, one week - what you'd make in a year in a miserable little shop. You'd be doing something special with your life, Alice. Rather than wasting your days trying to make ends meet. Worse still - having to explain yourself, and your past, for the rest of your life. You're better than that. You deserve better."

"But what you're asking me to do. It's wrong. Not to mention if I get caught that's my life over. It's too risky."

"Wrong? How is it wrong? The people who we'll be eradicating are scum. Druggies, corrupt politicians, dictators. Believe me, girl, we'll be doing the world a favour." He drummed his fingers on the steering wheel. "And you won't get caught. Not after I'm done training you."

They were getting close to home, passing alongside Rainham Marshes.

Alice swallowed. "If I say yes, what happens next?" Caesar grinned out the windscreen. "One step at a time, my dear. Why don't you get settled in tonight and meet me tomorrow? In town. We'll spend the day together. Do lunch." He glanced her up and down, raising an arched eyebrow at her tattered jeans and black overcoat. "We'll get you some new clothes as well."

They continued on the A13 for a while longer, before taking a right up the side of Old Dagenham Park. A few minutes later, Caesar pulled up outside Dagenham Heathway underground station.

"You can walk from here," he told her. "Tomorrow, you'll meet me outside the Intrepid Fox in Soho. At noon."

Alice glanced at him. "Yeah, okay. See you then. Thanks for the lift."

She got out and collected her sack of belongings from the back seat. She stood on the pavement and watched as the large car pulled away. Then she turned and headed for the station. Time to go home.

TWENTY

ALICE DIDN'T HAVE A KEY SO HAD TO RING THE BUZZER WHEN she got to the apartment block on the corner of Rockwell Road. There was no answer over the intercom. She buzzed again. Nothing.

"Come on, Mum, where are you?" She groaned, going for the buzzer again but knowing it was futile.

Next, she tried the buzzer of number twelve, the flat opposite - where Orla lived. She was a kind lady who Alice had spent a lot of time with growing up. She didn't have kids herself - she couldn't - and she'd been like a second mother to Alice. Grandma at least. Especially after Louisa began having men over at all hours of the day and night.

"Hello?" The muffled but familiar voice came over the intercom. "Who is it please?"

Alice sagged with relief. It was early in the day, but she was exhausted. A lot had happened since this morning.

"Orla. It's me. It's Alice."

The intercom went quiet. Then, "Alice? Really? You're home?"

"Yes, Mum's not answering. Can you let me in please?"

"Of course, one second."

Alice heard the receiver being replaced. Then a buzzer sounded, and the door clicked open. She entered the block and closed the door behind her. It felt weird to be back here but, at the same time, as though she'd never been away. The stairwell smelt the same - damp with a faint hint of room deodoriser. The bulb in the hallway was still out.

Alice ran up to the stairs to the first-floor and down to the end of the landing. Orla had already opened her door and was waiting to greet her.

"Oh, just look at yer," she drawled in her soft, Irish lilt. "All grown up. What a bonnie lass y'are, Alice."

Alice looked at the carpet. "It's good to see you. Do you still have a key to my place? My mum must be out."

Orla nodded. "Aye, I do. But come in and have a cup of tea with me first. Let's catch up."

Alice gripped her sack. She wanted a bath. Wanted to wash the smell of Crest Hill off her. But the way Orla was looking at her was too much.

"Yeah, that'd be nice," she said.

They went through and Alice got herself comfortable on the couch as Orla shuffled into the small kitchen area behind a half-partition wall. It was heartening to see the room was exactly how it had always been. Small figurines stood on nearly every surface, cherubic boys and girls playing with balls, skipping, sledging. Then there were the cat ornaments. A whole lot of cat ornaments.

"How long has it been?" Orla asked, placing a tray down on the coffee table. On it was a full matching tea set – pot, milk jug, sugar bowl, two dainty cups with saucers. Also on the tray, the obligatory plate of biscuits. Two digestives, two fig-rolls, and two chocolate fingers. The plate matched the tea set.

"I've been away three years," Alice told her. "Crazy, huh?"

Orla scowled. "It was disgusting what happened to you. Should never have been sent to that place." She turned to Alice with water eyes. "I'm sorry I didn't come to visit you, love. I meant to, but my legs have been bad. Louisa said it'd be best I stayed home. I didn't like that fella she was hanging around with I'll be honest with you. A fecking eejit he was."

Alice smiled. "I understand. It wasn't a nice place to visit. I'm home now."

"Yes. You are."

Orla poured out the tea and handed Alice a cup and saucer. Then she offered the plate of biscuits. Alice took a fig roll and placed it on the saucer.

"How has my mum been, these last few months?" she asked.

Orla's expression said it all. The deep sigh even more. "That bad?" Alice said.

"Have you noticed it as well?"

Alice traced her foot around the swirling pattern of Orla's carpet. "Sort of. She seems pretty forgetful and confused. About a lot of things. I thought she was drinking again. But it's not that, is it?"

Orla sipped her tea. Shook her head. "No. I don't think so. I'm sorry. I'll be honest with you now, Alice, I have been rather worried. These last few weeks especially."

"Is she getting worse?"

"She's not getting better."

They drank in silence a few minutes and Alice searched for something to say. A part of her was glad she wasn't imagining it, but it didn't help. Ever since she'd noticed her mum's confusion, she'd been looking in the library for reasons why. She'd even spoken to Jacqueline and Dr Richards about it. Alzheimer's was what they all suggested. It was getting a lot of press and seemed to be on the rise. There was no cure.

"What the hell can I do?" Alice murmured into the teacup.

Her mind drifted to Caesar and his offer of employment. Even if it was half what he suggested, it was a lot of money. She could get Louisa proper care. She was about to ask Orla about herself when they heard a commotion out in the corridor. The jangle of keys being dropped.

"Is that her?"

Alice was at the door in a second, her eagerness surprising even herself. She opened Orla's door to see her mum struggling with grocery bags.

"Mum," she cried. "I'm home."

Louisa spun around and for a second Alice's heart jumped into her neck. Did she even recognise her? But it wasn't that. Her open mouth was through shock. She dropped her bags and pulled Alice to her.

"My baby. Oh my God. My little baby is home." She was crying. Alice was crying. Behind her, Orla was crying as well. "How the hell? When?"

"They let me out early," Alice told her. "I thought they would have told you."

"No, they never."

"Doesn't matter. I'm here now."

They hugged each other tight, swaying together on the dark landing. Then Louisa unlocked the door to the flat, and they went in.

"Oh my god. I can't believe it," Louisa gasped. "What a treat. Are you okay my love? Can I get you a drink? Something to eat?"

Alice looked around the room. There was a new, bigger TV on the stand, new cushions on the couch, but otherwise, it was the way it had always been. They'd moved here when Alice was nine, after being forced out of their little house in Stockwell by developers. It wasn't the nicest flat in the world. But it was home.

She padded through into the kitchen and stood in the doorway, staring at the spot where it had happened. For the last few years, she'd dreaded this moment. But now, in the cold light of day, with the floor clean and the familiar smells of home in the air, she realised she felt nothing. She was numb to it. Oscar Duke was the past. He was gone. Dead.

"I am pretty hungry," Alice said. "A sandwich would be good. But I'll make it."

"Don't be daft, you sit down, I'll make it." Louisa scurried past her into the kitchen. She grabbed Alice by the shoulders and turned her around. "Why don't you go look at your old room. It's exactly how you left it."

"Yeah, I will. Thanks."

Alice picked up the blue plastic sack from the lounge and dragged it into the hallway. Her room lay at the end of the corridor, next to the bathroom. She smiled as she saw the large Velvet Underground poster was still on her door. Warhol's banana. She eased open the door and put her head around. The curtains were drawn like they always were, with a spike of late afternoon sun sheering through the gap, illuminating the space and highlighting a thin layer of dust which covered the surfaces. Her bed was still up against the far wall, its black and white striped duvet the same as when she'd left. The years had been less kind to the posters and magazine cuttings on her wall, which were now yellow and faded and the corners curled. She smiled at the photos of Bowie and Lou Reed, of Johnny Thunders and the Ramones and Ozzy. She'd forgotten many of the small details but being back in her room it almost felt like she'd never been away. With every gentle reminder of who she'd been before she was put inside, Crest Hill faded a little more.

She sat on her bed and breathed it in. Her room. Her safe space. She leaned over and switched on the portable stereo on her bedside table. Suicide's first album burst out of the small speakers. Alice nodded to herself and lay back on the bed. Everything was happening so fast, but it was so good to be home. Good to be lying on a real mattress instead of the thin, foam excuse for one she'd slept on these last few years. She closed her eyes as the throbbing synth-bass of Ghost Rider filled her consciousness.

There was a knock on the door. She rolled over and turned the music down. The door went again.

"Come in." She sat up and tucked her hair behind her ears.

"Here you go my angel," Alice's mum entered clutching a mug of tea. "Hot and sweet. As you like it."

Alice reached out for the drink. "Thanks, Mum." She paused. "I thought you were making me a sandwich?"

Louisa's face dropped. "Oh, yes, of course. Silly me. Where's my head at."

Alice put the tea down next to the stereo. "It's fine. I'll get something later. Sit down. Talk to me."

Louisa looked like a startled animal. Alice patted the duvet next to her, swung her feet onto the floor to make room.

Her mum dropped her hands into her lap. "I'm sorry, Sweetie. My mind is all over the place. I love you; you know."

Alice moved nearer and put her head on her shoulder. "I know."

They stayed like this for a while, their breathing falling in time with one another's. It was nice. But Alice knew she had to say it. She took a deep breath.

"Do you think you should see a doctor, Mum?"

Louisa didn't flinch. Alice held her nerve, resisting the desire to fill the silence. Her mum laughed.

"Whatever are you on about? Why do I need to see a doctor?"

"You've been getting confused, mum. Forgetting things. I noticed it a few months ago. Orla says it's been going on a while."

Louisa tutted, brusquely. "Bloody Orla, what the hell does she know? I haven't spoken to her properly in ages."

Alice looked at the ceiling and widened her eyes, defying the salty tears from falling. "I'm home now," she whispered into the room. "Whatever this is, we'll take care of it. I'm going to look after you." Louisa rested her head on Alice's. She knew. Alice could tell. She was scared.

"Oh love, what are we going to do?"

Alice wiped her eyes. "I'll get a job," she said. "A good job. I'll get us some money so we can get you the best medicine. Get you well. Okay? Whatever it takes."

She closed her eyes. Whatever it takes. She meant it. Even if that meant taking Beowulf Caesar up on his offer. Even if it meant she had to kill to get it.

TWENTY-ONE

ALICE HAD SLEPT SOUNDLY IN HER OLD BED BUT WOKE EARLY the next morning. She got out of bed and did her calisthenics program. Followed by stretches, a run around the estate, a shower. Then she got dressed and went through to the front room. Her mum was already up. She was sitting on the couch watching the news. She wore a matted old dressing gown and her hair stuck out like serpents.

"You want some breakfast, Sweetie?" she asked.

Alice sat on the side of the coffee table and pulled on her sixteen-hole Dr Martens.

"I already had a slice of toast," she said. "I'm going into town now. That okay?"

"Course it is. You want me to come with you?"

"No, you have a rest,' Alice told her, as she laced up her boots. 'I'm meeting some friends from school. Catching up. Then I'm going to go around a few bars and shops. See if I can get a job."

"Good girl." Louisa smiled. A full-faced, beaming smile. Full of pride. It made Alice feel worse.

"Do you want anything?" she asked.

"No. I've got everything I need now you're home."

Alice stood and grabbed her denim jacket. "Maybe tonight we can have a proper chat? About what we talked about last night. Are you still with Dr Raheem?"

Her mum frowned. "I don't want to be a bother, love. I'm a bit stressed. But I'm fine."

Alice stared at her. "I think it'd be good for you to get checked out. Please? For me?"

"Fine,' Louisa said. 'I suppose it's nice you care. But I promise - there's nothing wrong with me."

"All right, mum. Well, I'll see you later. Have a good day." She stopped at the door and went back, kissed Louisa on the cheek. "It is good to be home."

"It's good to have you home. I love you, Sweetie."

"I love you too," Alice mumbled, then she hurried out the door before the quivering sensation in her stomach morphed into anything too embarrassing.

Outside the streets were quiet, the air still. Alice walked slowly, reacquainting herself with the sights and smells of Reede Road. The fresh air on her skin was glorious. She got to the end of the street and took a left down Heathway, heading to the underground.

Once there she jumped on the District Line to Mile End then changed to the Central line for Oxford Circus. The journey took around an hour and gave Alice time to reflect. To come to terms with the last twenty-four hours. Her mum's condition. Caesar's offer. She knew he'd want an answer and she couldn't mess him around.

She left the underground and hurried along Wardour Street to the rendezvous. It was lunchtime and the area was packed with people. Tourists and sightseers brushing shoulders with market traders and locals in a weird dichotomy of worlds. It was apparent elsewhere in the centre but nowhere as concentrated as in Soho.

Alice saw Beowulf Caesar before he saw her. He was waiting outside the Intrepid Fox, as arranged. He was wearing the same fur-collared leather coat as before, but this time with a royal blue suit underneath, complemented with a bright, neon orange tie and matching socks. He watched people as they passed by, a perma-sneer playing across his wide face. He looked up, saw Alice, and his face cracked into a broad smile.

"Here she is. The woman of the hour." He held his arms out wide and gestured to the sky. "Your first real day of freedom. Feels bleeding beautiful, doesn't it?"

"I'm okay," she said, shrugging. "Not done much yet. But I'm here. What we doing?"

"*What we doing?*" Caesar mocked. "Come on, kiddo, you're better than that. We've got an electrifying day ahead of us." He looked Alice up and down. "Starting with buying you some new threads, I'd say?"

Twenty minutes later and they were on a packed tour of Oxford Street's finer establishments. John Lewis, House of Fraser, Selfridges. In Zara Alice tried on a pair of black jeans.

"You like those?" Caesar asked, as she pulled back the curtain on the changing room and stepped out.

Alice twisted her hips, looking at the jeans in the mirror. "Yeah, I do. But they're seventy-quid."

Caesar scoffed. "We'll get you two pairs then. Go on, give us a twirl." His teeth glinted under the bright halogen bulbs. Alice hesitated a second but did as she was told. "Lovely arse, haven't you?"

"What? No." Alice looked at the floor, feeling her cheeks burn.

"Calm it down, darling. I'm not trying it on." Caesar got up from the low leather couch he'd been reclining on and moved towards her. Put a big hand on each shoulder. "Just sizing up the possibilities. My investment. Brains and beauty. That's how you get them."

"Get who?"

"Anyone you bloody well need to." He spun Alice around and stood behind her, resting his chin on her head and both looking into the changing room mirror. "Look at you. You're dynamite, Alice. I made a good decision with you. So, are we buying these jeans, or what?"

The shopping expedition carried on for the next few hours, ending in Harrods where they spent time on each level.

Alice had never been in Harrods before - never had any desire to visit - but now, with Caesar and his American Express card, it was like a paradise. In the clothing department she tried on four leather jackets, all of which Caesar offered to buy her, but none of them were quite right. Instead, Alice settled for two black blouses - one in denim and one a kind of viscose silk. She also picked out three t-shirts and a Vivienne Westwood bracelet that cost more than anything Alice had ever owned. Caesar bought himself a white shirt with red leather wingtips on the collar and a black trilby with a red silk band.

As they walked around Alice enjoyed the looks on people's faces as they passed by. The young goth girl and the thug-queen. They laughed together, tried on clothes, took the piss out of people. They made a good team.

"I don't know about you, darling, but I'm famished," Caesar bellowed once they'd racked up another few hundred in the shoe department - a pair of eight-hole, cherry Dr Marten's for Alice, some Kurt Geiger slip-ons for Caesar. "What's say we get some food?"

"Yeah. That'd be good," Alice said. "Where do you want to go? There's a McDonald's a few blocks away I think."

Caesar tutted camply. "Not a bleeding chance. But don't worry, I know just the place."

TWENTY-TWO

THE IVY WAS CROWDED — EVEN FOR A TUESDAY AFTERNOON - but the austere waiter found them a table straight away. A booth in the far corner, away from the large, central bar. Alice stared, unblinking, as they were led through the extravagant dining room. On each table lavishly dressed people sipped expensive wine, forking lettuce leaves into their perfect mouths. Alice was shocked at how quiet the room was. A dull murmur of well-spoken voices bubbling over the noise of cutlery and the chink of wine glasses.

The waiter seated them and returned a few moments later with menus.

"What's the special today, old boy?" Caesar asked, winking at Alice.

The waiter straightened himself. "Today we have crayfish-tail linguine with rocket and truffle oil. Topped with an herb and garlic crumb."

"Yes. We'll both have the special, merci," Caesar said. "And a bottle of Cristal."

The waiter raised his eyebrows. "Very good sir."

He shuffled off. Alice watched as he wound stealthily around a table inhabited by a tanned man in his fifties and a beautiful younger woman with long red hair. Alice recognised them both but wasn't sure from where. Actors maybe.

She turned back to Caesar.

"You like it here?" he asked.

Alice chewed her lip. "Yeah – I mean, yes, thank you - it's amazing. Bit posh though, isn't it?"

"Well, get used to it. This could be your life from now on. Eating in the best restaurants, drinking the finest champagne. Wearing the best clothes. Even if everything is bloody black." He burst out laughing but stopped quickly as a new waiter arrived with a bottle of champagne and two glasses. He showed the bottle to Caesar who waved him away and told him to pour. The waiter twisted the cork and held it clandestinely in his hand as it came out with a pop, then with one hand behind his back he filled Alice's glass, letting the bubbles subside before topping up. Alice watched all this with a smile on her face. So much pomp and she loved it.

"Go on, don't wait for me," Caesar said. "Have a go"

Tentatively Alice took a sip. It tasted like lemonade, only more sour. It was nice enough.

"Louis Roederer Cristal," Caesar growled as the waiter finished filling his own glass. "Received a hundred-point score in the trade magazines two years ago."

"Does that mean it's good?"

"It means it's the best," Caesar said, showing his gold teeth. "Enjoy."

The waiter placed the bottle in a silver bucket next to

the table and disappeared into the sea of tables. Caesar waited a moment then looked at Alice. All the humour drained from his face.

"Down to business then," he whispered, a gruffness now in his tone. "Here's what's on the table. You'll work for me, in my new organisation. I've got a crack team already assembled but I need one more. Maybe two. And you fit the bill perfectly. I want you to be part of this, Alice. All this today, it's a sweetener sure, but it's also a glimpse of what your life can be like. You'll be paid five grand per job initially, but my projections are that's going to rise exponentially once we become industry leaders."

Alice drank back a bigger mouthful. Five grand. That was more money than she'd ever seen. "But you'd want me to – kill people?"

Caesar leaned forward. "Keep your voice down." He sat back, composed himself. "I like to think we're providing a service. Removing problems. Eradicating troublesome pests. But yes. If you want to be gauche about it, that's what it boils down to."

Alice's heart thumped against her ribs. "But I wouldn't know how."

"Well, that's not true is it,' Caesar replied. "I heard all about your escapades inside. You took some bitches eye for Christ's sake." He smirked, drinking. "Fucking beautiful."

"But what if I get caught. Or get myself killed, I couldn't…"

Caesar held his hand up and she trailed off. The waiter had arrived with their meals. A steaming bowl of pasta with dainty pieces of fried fish and what looked like little lobster tails. The smell was amazing.

"Don't you worry about all that," Caesar continued, once the waiter had left. "You'll be trained up. Given everything you need to become the person you need to become. And you'll get there quickly, I can tell. But for now, all I need by the end of the day is yes, or no." And with that, he picked up his fork and greedily attacked his bowl of food.

TWENTY-THREE

THE AFTERNOON FOLLOWED A SIMILAR TRAJECTORY AS THE morning, which meant more shopping, but electronics this time. Caesar bought Alice a laptop and an iPod, which she was excited about. They'd been released while she was inside, and she'd heard lots of good things about them. She told Caesar how grateful she was. How she couldn't wait to get home and give it a try. By this stage, the day was drawing to a close, but Caesar suggested they grab a cocktail before parting ways.

"I don't know," Alice told him. "My mum will be wondering where I am."

Thew truth was she still felt light-headed after drinking half a bottle of expensive champagne, but Caesar insisted, dragging her playfully into a wine bar off Old Compton Street.

"Sit down, I'll get them." He walked her over to a table along one wall and placed his many shopping bags down. "Martini's all round?"

Alice placed her pile of shopping down and sat on a low stool. "Yeah sure."

She watched as Caesar strutted towards the bar at the far end of the room. With his swagger and other-worldly superiority. He was like a rock star. Confidence and charisma oozed from him. But as Alice sat there, she wondered, could she work for someone like him? More importantly - could she kill for him?

"There you are, my dear."

Alice's daydream broke as Caesar placed a drink down in front of her. It was one of those classic cocktail glasses with slanted sides. Like in the movies. The glass was frosted and the liquid inside was crystal clear. Leaning against the side of the glass, a thin wooden cocktail stick held three bulbous green olives.

"Thank you," Alice mumbled. She lifted the glass carefully up to her lips and took a sip. It was ice cold and tasted horrible.

Caesar laughed. "You'll get a taste for it. Believe me."

"Shaken not stirred," Alice replied.

"Not a chance. James bleeding Bond? What a fucking drip. No, Doll. These are *Gin* Martinis. Stirred slowly, over ice. The only way to go." He took a long drink and smacked his lips like before. "So then, my little angel in black. Time for you to make your decision. Is it a yes or a no?"

Alice put her glass down and took a deep breath. But before she had a chance to speak a man appeared beside their table.

'All right, Ceez?' He leaned over and placed his arm around Caesar's broad shoulders before stage-whispering in his ear, "Want to go to the bathroom?"

He was tall and muscular with a shaved head, and had on blue jeans, ripped at the knees. On his top half, he wore a blue denim shirt with the top few buttons open to reveal a tattoo on his clavicle bone of the word *Tony*.

Caesar cleared his throat but didn't look at the man. His eyes, a second ago full of mirth and charm were now cold and cruel. His mouth twisted into a nasty sneer as he addressed Alice. "Excuse me, sweetie. Won't be a moment."

He got to his feet and faced the man. "Why don't we go outside?"

The man grinned, drunkenly. "Sure, if that's what you want. There's a private yard around the back."

Caesar smiled, but only with his mouth, and even then, only a hint. "Lead the way," he said.

He cast Alice a glance before following the man out the door. Through the window, she saw them take a right and then disappear. Turning back to her drink, she took another sip. The pressure in her head was back and her veins pulsed with nervous tension. There was something about the look Caesar had given her just now. It made her uneasy.

She gulped down another mouthful of Martini and got to her feet. Her next thought was, what to do with the shopping bags, but she decided they'd be safe. Everyone had seen them arrive and she assumed no one would be dumb enough to steal from Caesar. Hurrying out of the wine bar, she made her way down the adjacent alleyway, heading towards the rear of the building. There was no one in sight but she could hear voices and the sound of movement.

At the end of the narrow passage, it opened out into a small courtyard that belonged to the wine bar. A large refuse bin, overflowing with empty bottles stood against the nearside wall and Alice moved over to it, edging around the back to peer into the yard. She didn't yet have eyes on Caesar and the other man, but she could hear them, could hear panting and gasping, the sound of something heavy hitting the floor. Then as she peered around, she saw Caesar's huge frame. He had his back to her, but she could see his whole upper body was twisted and tense. On the floor in front of him knelt the man from the bar. He looked up and noticed Alice as she moved further into the space. He held his arms out. Pleading. His face was bloody and bruised like he'd already taken a firm pounding.

"Help," he croaked. "Please…"

Before he could finish, Caesar smashed a large, heavy-ringed fist into his face, busting open his nose on impact. The man slumped forward, but Caesar grabbed him around the throat and lifted him upright. Blood gushed down his face into his red, swollen mouth.

"Who the hell do you think you are?" Caesar snarled, through gritted teeth. "I am not someone you sidle up to like some cheap queen."

He let go of the man's throat and he wilted to the ground. Alice was hoping this would now be the end of it, but next Caesar raised his foot and stamped his full weight onto the man's guts.

"No—"

She clasped her hands to her mouth as Caesar spun around and glared at her. She stared back at him. Frozen. Uncertain as to what to do.

"Come here," Caesar beckoned her over. "I said come here." His voice softened and held his arm out to her.

"Listen, Alice. This isn't how I do things. But this pathetic puff should have known better."

Alice shuffled over, glancing from Caesar to the man. He looked to be dead. "Who is he?" she asked.

"He's no one," Caesar snarled. "An ex. Sort of. Someone who should know better. Embarrassing me like that in public."

Alice's stomach reeled, and it wasn't just the Martini. What she'd done to Big Ella, to Oscar Duke, it had always seemed to her to be honourable. A form of righteous justice. But this was something else.

"You have a go," Caesar growled. "Those boots look like they could do some damage. Finish him off." Alice froze. The man was making strange guttural noises. Like a dying animal. Caesar laid a heavy hand on her shoulder. 'Go on, my girl."

"I can't," she whispered.

"Yes, Alice. You can. You're a killer. A cold-hearted killer. I know it." Caesar stepped over to the man's prone form and turned around to face her. He raised his foot in the air and looked her dead in the eyes. "Just like me."

He stamped down on the man's head with his big size twelve foot. Alice looked away in time. Heard a terrible splintering sound.

That was enough.

Fighting for air she hurried back up the dark alley. She was going to throw up. She was going to pass out. She did neither.

As she got to the end of the alley, she could hear Caesar behind her. Telling her to come back. Telling her if she walked away, she was on her own.

But she didn't stop.

The bats screamed in her head as she quickened her pace, taking a left down Wardour Street and over into China Town.

Her senses were heightened and on overdrive. It was early evening, and the area was packed with tourists and diners. She ducked down the side of the Lotus Garden and hid in a doorway to regain her composure. Once away from the crowds she closed her eyes, did the breath-counting exercise Jacqueline had taught her. After a few minutes she felt less hysterical, less like her head might explode.

She covered her face with her hands. Had he planned that somehow? Was it some macabre way of testing her?

She let out a deep sigh. If it was a test, she'd failed. But of course she had. She'd been stupid to even consider what Caesar was asking of her. She wasn't a killer. She was a young girl, fighting for survival. She'd done bad stuff, sure, but she didn't have to keep on doing it. She had a choice.

Resolute now, she set off home. Today had been fun, exciting even. But she couldn't do it. Couldn't become the person Caesar wanted her to be. She was adamant now. It was decided. She'd get her head down. Get a job. Live a decent life. She might not ever be rich, or even happy, but she'd be free.

TWENTY-FOUR

THE TV WAS ON IN THE FRONT ROOM AS ALICE ENTERED the flat. She could see the orange light leaking out under the door and spreading at a sharp angle up the hallway wall. Her first thought was to go straight to her room. But as she tip-toed past the lounge door she heard another sound over the dull hum of the TV. Crying.

She cracked open the door to see her mum sitting on the floor with her back to the couch. She was surrounded by bits of paper and in her hand was a large glass of clear liquid. Vodka, at a guess. She'd also been smoking. And heavily, from the number of butts in the overflowing ashtray. She'd told Alice she'd quit.

"Mum? What's happened?" She went through as Louisa looked up. Long thick tracks of mascara ran down both cheeks.

She sniffed back. "I'm all right, love." She pointed at the TV. "Just a sad film."

Alice glanced at the screen. Richard Gere in something she didn't recognise. "What are all these?"

Her mum tried to gather up the papers, but Alice was too quick. She grabbed at two of the sheets and held them up. Scanned the information. They were bailiff letters. It didn't look good.

"Oh shit, mum. Why didn't you say something?"

Louisa took a long drink. She pulled a packet of Richmond Menthols from her pocket and slid one out. Still elegantly as ever she pushed it between her lips and lit it up.

"I'm sorry, Sweetie. I didn't want to bother you. It's been building up a few months, maybe more." She took a long drag of the cigarette. "I've not had anything coming in for a while. Not since Steve left. I'm getting too old for this game. No one wants me."

A surge of anger hit Alice in the chest. "What do you mean? You can do other things. I don't want you doing that anyway. You could work in a shop or a bar like other people do. That's my plan."

"Don't you think I've tried, Al?" she said. "It seems my reputation proceeds me around these parts. The looks I got in some places. No one wants an old slapper working for them."

Alice glared. "Don't call yourself that."

"It's what I am, isn't it? What people will always see me as." She pushed back against the couch and got to her feet. "It's not just that though, sweetie." She walked through to the kitchen and opened the drawer under the microwave. She removed a thin brown envelope and brought it back into the lounge. Handed it to Alice. "I'm sorry, my love. I wanted to protect you from all this. But you should know, I suppose. It's going to affect us both."

Alice held the envelope in her hands for a moment, then backed away and sat in the armchair facing the couch. She turned the envelope over.

"What is it?"

Her mum waved her cigarette at the envelope. "Read it."

Alice slipped the white paper out and unfolded it on her lap. It was from the hospital. Results of an MRI scan on her mum's brain. It said they'd discovered blood vessel damage, as well as shrinkage in the frontal and temporal lobes.

Alice looked up. "What does it mean mum?"

"Alzheimer's, they call it. Dr Raheem said it explains why I've been a bit scatty lately. Said it might also explain some of my more – impulsive - behaviours over the last few years. It builds up slow."

Alice wiped the heel of her hand across her eye. "What can we do?"

"We can't do anything. I've been reading up on it. I'm just going to get worse. Could be in a few years, could be a lot longer, but eventually I won't remember who I am. Who you are." This set her off. Loud gushing sobs. Tears and snot and anguish.

Alice went to her. Held her. She didn't have any words, but no words mattered. "What can I do?" she asked, once they'd both cried themselves dry.

Louisa pulled away and sat on the couch. "Not sure. We'll be evicted soon. I owe money left right and centre. I'm so sorry, my angel."

Alice was quiet. The chatter of the bats was loud in her head but there was something else present now too. The fat manatee of despair making its presence known. Sitting heavy on her shoulders, weighing her down.

"Can I have one of those?" she asked, nodding at the packet of Richmond's.

"You don't smoke."

"Yeah, well maybe I do now."

Louisa removed one of the cigarettes and handed it to her. Followed by the red plastic lighter. Alice sparked it up and inhaled deeply, holding the hot smoke in her lungs before blowing a large cloud into the room.

She stood up. "I need a drink as well. Usual place?"

Her mum feigned shock a moment, then nodded. Alice walked into the kitchen and opened the bottom cupboard, pulled out the bottle of Smirnoff from behind the cereal boxes. She reached up and got a glass from the shelves next to the cooker and poured herself a generous measure. Drank it down in one. Didn't taste it. She poured out another and went back through into the lounge.

"I'll get a job, mum," she said, sitting next to her. "I'll do whatever it takes."

She thought of Caesar and a wave of self-loathing washed over her. She'd messed everything up. Just like she always did. Caesar had promised her a retainer, for whilst she trained. Twenty-grand. She could have paid her mum's debts off in a second.

"You're a good girl," her mum said, putting her head on her Alice's shoulder. "I'm so proud of you." The words felt like hot knives in her heart.

"I'm not a good girl, mum."

They sat together and stared at the TV for a while until

Alice realised her mum had fallen asleep. Gently she got up, and laid her down on the couch, stuffing a cushion under her head. Then she kissed her on the forehead.

"I will look after you," she whispered. "I'll make this okay. I promise."

TWENTY-FIVE

ALICE DIDN'T SLEEP WELL. HER MIND WAS A MESS OF IDEAS and her heart heavy with regret. By morning her whole body burned with a deep rage. At life. At her mum's rotten predicament. At the fact she'd cut off their only lifeline.

She washed and dressed and went through to the lounge. The TV was off, and her mum was nowhere to be seen. She made herself a slice of toast and ate it standing in the kitchen. Then she straightened the couch, removed the TV remote from down the back of a cushion, and placed it on the coffee table. The bailiff letters were still strewn around the carpet. She gathered them into a pile and left them on the coffee table. Next to them, she left a short note, telling her mum she was going to be out all day. Job hunting. Then she grabbed her black hoodie and denim jacket and left.

Outside the day was miserable. A harsh wind whipped Alice's hair onto her cheeks as she struggled down the high street, ducking into shops along the way. In each establishment she put on her poshest voice, the one she'd been practicing. Asked politely but confidently if they had any work available. Some were polite back, some sniffed a curt response, but the answer was the same. No jobs. No work.

Disheartened, but not giving up, Alice jumped the tube barrier and rode the line to Whitechapel. She'd made this part of East London her stomping ground as a teenager, and she hoped the hip bars and vintage shops here would be more inclined to hire someone like her.

She ambled her way along Brick Lane and headed up towards Shoreditch. In each establishment, she waited patiently at the counter or the bar, asking politely when asked if she could speak to the manager. Hell, she even flirted a little when she thought it might help her case. But like before she came out jobless each time. Some told her to come back at the weekend when management would be there, others said to drop a CV in and they'd have a look at it. The problem was Alice didn't have a CV and didn't have anything to put on a CV. She was in the middle of a terrible vicious circle, of which she could see no way of getting out.

By lunchtime, the pressure in her head had become too much. Sounds were muffled and a string of intrusive thoughts had her worried. In one newsagent she distracted the man behind the counter enough to reach over and steal a packet of ten cigarettes and a box of matches. She pocketed them and hurried out of the shop.

Exhausted and despondent she found a bench facing the side entrance of Spitalfields Market and took out the box of cigarettes. Embassy Number Ones. She peeled the cellophane cover from the end.

"Load of bullshit," she snarled to herself. "How are you supposed to get by in this stupid life?"

She flipped open the end of the cigarette box and pulled out the silver paper, followed by one of the smokes. She jammed it between her lips and took out the box of matches. They were standard, rather than safety matches. She scraped a match along the side of the box, delighting somewhat as the flame burst forth. She lifted it up to light the cigarette, but before she had a chance the wind blew it out.

"Balls."

She tried again, same thing. And again. By the fifth attempt, she'd lost patience. With a grunt, she threw the box of matches across the street. Then she sat back and sucked on the dry cigarette, defeated.

"Need a light?"

She looked up into the speaker's face, a man in his mid-twenties, stocky, with a shaved head. Not her type, at all, but he had a certain twinkle in his eyes. A certain cocksure charm about him.

"Can I sit down?" he asked, offering her a silver lighter.

Alice took it and lit the cigarette greedily. "It's a free country."

"That it is."

He sat as Alice handed back the lighter. He slipped a pack of twenty from his coat pocket and lit one himself. Alice stared forward, but out of the corner of one eye, she noticed a tattoo on his inner forearm. Some sort of military insignia. A quote in Latin.

He turned to Alice. "You look like you've got the weight of the world on your shoulders."

Alice shrugged. "Feels like I have."

"Want to talk about it?"

"Not to you, no."

The man leaned in. "I'm a good listener. Names Pete, by the way." He held out his hand. Alice ignored it. "Come on, love. What's a pretty girl like you got to be sad about?"

Alice rolled her eyes. This was the last thing she needed. "Hey, I'm talking to you," Pete snapped, his tone

changing. "You're being rude."

"No, I'm not," Alice said. "You are. I was sitting here minding my own business. I didn't ask you for a light. I certainly didn't ask you to join me. So please, leave me alone."

Pete laughed. A shrill, mocking type of laugh. The sort of laugh the boys in Alice's old class would do if any of the girls tried to stick up for themselves. She hated people like this. Bullies.

Pete didn't make to go. So they both sat in silence. Alice felt nervous. Uncomfortable. But she wasn't going to back down. She wasn't going to be the one to move. Then Pete put his hand on her thigh.

"Hey. Get off," Alice cried. She tried to pull away, but he gripped her tighter, moving his rough, calloused hand up between her legs. "Get the fuck off me!' Alice yelled, louder now. She pushed against Pete, but he wouldn't let go. In the end, she jammed the lit end of her cigarette into the back of Pete's hand. He let go when she did that. But laughing. Wanting her to know it had been his choice.

Alice jumped to her feet. "Wanker."

"Ah piss off, you frigid cow." Pete went back to his cigarette, as though nothing had happened. Alice turned on her heels and scurried away down the side of the market building. She was shaking. She didn't slow down until she got to Liverpool Street Station.

Bitter tears stung her eyes as she made her way down the escalator. She jumped the barrier and got on the Central line to Oxford Circus. From there it was a short walk to Soho. She hadn't articulated it to herself at all, but she knew where she was heading. Knew why.

As Alice neared the bar where she'd last seen Caesar, she saw the police tape. Saw the sign. Closed until further notice. No surprise there. Keeping her head down, she moved on, drifting from bar to restaurant to bar, peering through steamy windows into gloomy establishments, hoping to spot the unmistakable form of Beowulf Caesar. But he was nowhere to be found.

By the time she got to the Intrepid Fox, it was 7 p.m and already dark. She hung around outside for a few minutes, stamping her feet to ward off the cold. She could hear music drifting out from inside the pub, Bodies by the Sex Pistols, followed by a live version of some Guns and Roses song. Alice wasn't a big fan of either, but the music was loud and nihilistic, and it fitted her mood perfectly. It told her, 'Come on in, drink away your sorrows.'

She certainly wanted to. But she had no money. Same as always. Instead, she kicked her heels a while down the side of the block before taking a shortcut through the back of Soho Square. The plan now was to get to Tottenham Court tube station and get back home. She was done. In every conceivable way.

TWENTY-SIX

SOHO GARDENS WAS DESERTED AS ALICE PASSED THROUGH. Dusk was turning into night and a bristle of something like anxiety tickled the hair on her neck. She heard a noise behind her. Footsteps, maybe. She spun around. No one in sight. She paused a moment. Scanned the streets and the alleyways, either side of her. Nothing. Head down she hurried onwards, through the square and down the street on the other side. Here too there was no one around. A sinister sensation hung in the air. Like the lull before an electric storm. She could sense something bad was about to happen. Up ahead were the lights of the main street. She was almost there. But coming towards her were a group of three men in their early thirties. They were drunk, rowdy, singing football songs. Alice halted. She could handle them of course, but emotionally she felt raw. A better option was an alley that cut through to the next street along. It was dark, but if she went quick, she'd be through in a minute or so. She decided to risk it.

"Well, well, well. Look who we have here."

She was only a few steps into the alley when she heard the voice behind her. She twisted around and her heart fell into her guts. The horrible prick from earlier. Pete.

"You followed me?"

Pete leered at her. "Maybe I did. Maybe I wanted to see how far I could take this."

Alice turned to run. But he grabbed her by the wrist and pulled her to him. With his other hand, he grabbed her around the neck and slammed her against the wall.

"Think you're better than me. Do you?" He rasped in Alice's ear. Spit slid down her cheek. "Well, you're not. You're a cheap skank."

Alice grappled at his hand around her throat. "What do you want?" She could hardly get her words out. "Let me go, please."

Pete's eyes widened. "Nah. Sorry love. Not happening." He reached around and got something out of his pocket. Alice heard the click. Saw the blade reflected in the moonlight. Pete held the knife edge against her cheek. "Be a shame if someone was to ruin that pretty face of yours, hey?"

Alice tensed at the pressure of the blade on her face. They remained there a moment. Frozen in time. The only sound was their breath. Quick, shallow. Then, suddenly there was a noise further down the alley. A cat maybe, or a London rat. It didn't matter. In that split-second, Pete was distracted. He dropped his guard and Alice saw her chance. She brought her knee up and connected hard with his groin, feeling the squelch of his balls against his pelvic bone. As he doubled over in pain, Alice's first instinct was to run, to remove herself from the situation and not stop until she was safe. But then another drive took over. Something stronger. A deep, body rage swelled inside of her as the bats screamed for blood.

Destroy, they told her.

Kill.

Alice raised her elbow and brought it down hard on the back of Pete's neck. He was still bent over, holding his groin and the blow knocked him to the floor. Once there Alice kicked him as hard as she could in the face. Finally, a reason for the steel-toecaps she always paid extra for. His nose exploded on impact, and she felt some teeth go as well.

But he was a tough one, was Pete. No doubt ex-military, as the tattoo suggested. He grabbed at Alice's ankle, slashing wildly at her with the knife, still clenched tight in his fist. Alice evaded the weapon, dancing around with her free leg before administering another swift kick to the sternum. He stumbled back, winded. But it didn't stop him. Alice went again with a kick to the stomach. And another. She heard the knife clatter to the floor as he released her. Now was the time to run. To not look back. To escape.

But Alice stayed.

The bats were in charge.

In one fluid move, she grabbed for the knife before dropping heavily, straddling her attacker's lower torso. With grunt from her and a groan from him she stabbed the blade into his chest. Straight down, through his ribs. Into his heart. He stared up at her with a shocked expression on his face, tried to say something, but blood was gurgling from his throat and choking him. He looked scared. Then he laughed. Then he went limp.

Alice clambered to her feet. It was dark, but she could

see well enough to know she was covered in Pete's blood. Her hands were covered in it, she could feel it on her face. Then, as her awareness spread, she heard a police siren. It sounded to be a way off, but it was getting closer. She wrapped her jacket around her and hurried down to the end of the alley. She peered left and right up the road, no one around. She pulled her hood up, shoved her sticky hands in her pockets, and set off walking towards Tottenham Court Road.

She was unsure what she was going to do when she got to the bright unforgiving lights of the tube station, but her hope was she could slip through without anyone noticing her. But that plan crumbled to dust as a police car turned down the end of the street and flashed its lights.

"Shit!"

Alice stopped and then turned around, feigned as though she'd forgotten something, and headed in the opposite direction. She quickened her pace but resisted the temptation to run. Her heart beat fast in her chest. The pulse points in her legs and neck throbbed.

They aren't looking for you, she told herself. It was a routine patrol. That was all. But they were closing in. A few seconds more and they'd be alongside her. Would see the blood on her clothes. On her face. She got to the end of the street and took a left. Out of the corner of her eye she saw another car drive past. Saw it stop. She kept going. Behind her she heard the car again. Shit. It had turned around. She walked faster.

"Going my way darling."

Alice's stomach did a somersault. She looked around to

see Caesar's big face peering out the back window of the car. "Get in. Now. Otherwise, you're screwed."

Alice stopped. The police car was at the end of the street. The right indicators flashed. They were coming her way.

"You don't want to be explaining to the filth why you're covered in claret, do you?" Caesar growled. "Get in the car, Alice. Don't be a fool."

He opened the door and shuffled over to let her in. She gave the police car one last glance then jumped in beside him.

"Okay, Davros," Caesar barked. "Get us out of here."

Alice held onto the door handle as the man driving twisted the steering wheel around and did a sharp U-turn before speeding off in the opposite direction. She looked back over her shoulder, watching as the police car stopped. She held her breath. Froze. But then the brake lights went off and it continued on its way.

"Wasn't that a close call?" Caesar said. "Lucky for you we drove past when we did."

All Alice could do was nod. She might have been in shock, she wasn't sure. She looked down at her hands. The blood was already dry and had turned a dirty brown colour. She rubbed them on her jeans before Caesar tutted loudly and handed her a packet of baby wipes.

"Thank you," Alice managed. "How did you know?" Caesar looked right at her. "I cannot tell a lie, my dear.

We were following you. Thought it'd be savvy of me to see what you were up to. Work out a way to change your mind. I was going to apologise for you having to see all that unpleasantness yesterday, but then again," he looked her up and down and pursed his lips. "Seems you're quite happy to be just as unpleasant yourself."

The man driving laughed. Alice frowned at the back of his head.

"I was defending myself. That's all."

"Is that right, Chuck?" the driver said, in a soft Northern accent. "I hear you do a lot of that - defending yourself. Often ends up with someone else dead though, from what I hear."

Caesar cleared his throat. "Where are my manners. Alice, let me introduce you to one of my best friends and associates, now known as Davros Ratpack."

The man, Davros Ratpack, turned around and kissed the air. "Charmed, I'm sure. I've been looking forward to meeting this golden girl."

Alice eyed him up and down. He was wide and toned, with short, bleached hair that was gelled forward over a heavily made-up face. Eyeliner, blusher, an inch of foundation. More make-up than Alice ever wore herself. Though it suited him. She couldn't see his bottom half from where she was sitting, but on his top, he wore a plaid lumberjack shirt with the sleeves cut off.

"I have heard a lot about you as it happens," he went on. "All of it good by the way. I'm looking forward to working with you."

Alice shot a look at Caesar. He grinned back, enjoying the exchange.

"You still want me to work for you?"

Caesar sat back and gazed out the window. He didn't look at her when he said, "Training will start tomorrow and will last three months. Once it starts that'll be it. No going back. Literally." He looked at her. Right in the eyes. "From that point on you'll cut all ties with your past. Understood? While you train, you'll be known only as a number. You'll be Six. Once training is done, you'll choose your new name. Any questions?"

Alice held his gaze. "What about my mum?"

Caesar shook his head. "You'll cut all ties. Say your goodbyes tonight and Alice Vandella will be gone. Dead. I've got the best people. Once I give them the go ahead, they'll orchestrate your death, create the right document. A few years down the line they'll systematically sweep every database, all records. Delete any mention of you. It'll be like you never existed."

"But my mum isn't well. I need to care for her." She coughed, composed herself. "I'm sorry. I can't leave her."

Caesar closed his eyes and breathed out slowly down his nose. "Fine. Davros can drop you out now. Leave you for the filth to pick up." He shook his head. "Shame, though. A man dead. You covered in his blood. You'll be back in borstal by the weekend. Actually no, it'll be prison for you now. A life sentence, I'd bet. Not sure how you look after your old mum when you're locked up. But there you go."

Alice shivered. She didn't know what to say. The world was closing in on her. She wanted to scream. Wanted to smash her fist into something.

"All sounds pretty shitty does that, boss," Davros Ratpack butted in. "Is there no other way?"

"Thank you for asking Davros," Caesar replied, playing it straight. "I think there might be another way. What about this?"

He placed a brown paper bag on Alice's lap. She slowly

opened it up to see there were three large wads of notes at the bottom. All fifties.

"Ten grand," Caesar said. "Call it a relocation package."

"For me?"

"For you. I'd say you can get your mum whatever help she needs. As I've already explained, you'll get paid to train and then be on commission once you're in the field." He leaned over to her, smiling. "Now all you have to do is tell me you're in."

Alice swallowed. "All right," she whispered. "I'm in." Caesar sat back and laughed. A loud, affected laugh.

Slapped the back of Davros's seat. "Bloody good show. I knew you'd make the right decision in the end. She's going to love her new job. Don't you think Davros?"

"Absolutely C. No question." He turned around and winked at Alice. "Just you wait, Chuck. You won't know what's hit you. It's going to be murderous."

TWENTY-SEVEN

DAVROS DROPPED ALICE OFF AT DAGENHAM HEATHWAY. HE had offered to take her all the way home, but she wanted the walk. She needed some fresh air, time to think. But mainly she didn't want Orla or her mum to see her travelling companions. Her new colleagues.

She climbed out of the car and stood on the side of the road with her arms folded. "What happens next?"

Caesar handed her a piece of paper. "Be at this address at eleven, tomorrow morning. Bring clothes, a few belongings. But not too much."

Alice snorted down her nose. "I haven't got much."

"That's fine. As I said, once you're in, there's no coming back. Say your goodbyes tonight, however you need to. But I hope it goes without saying, don't bleeding well mention where you're going and what you're doing. And don't mention me."

Alice took the note. "Sure."

"See you tomorrow, Six. Sleep well."

The car window whirred close. Alice watched the car as

it cruised to the end of the road. Then it indicated left and disappeared. She remained there a few seconds as the enormity of what had transpired over the last few hours hit her. She could still see Pete's face when she closed her eyes. Could still recall the heady cocktail of emotions. Rage. Fear. Dread. She looked down at her hands, the blood remained in the lines of her knuckles, under her fingernails. She'd killed someone. What's more, she'd signed up to do the exact same thing for the rest of her life.

Alice's front room window was visible from the road but as she got nearer, she saw the lights were off. Not even the multi-coloured glow of a TV on. Alice hurried up the path and let herself in.

"Mum? I'm home," she called as she opened the door to flat eleven. "You in?"

There was no answer. Alice switched on the living room light and went through to the kitchen. She opened the fridge and took out a bottle of fresh orange. It was out of date, but she twisted off the top and took a large gulp regardless. It tasted fizzy. Wasn't supposed to. She replaced it and went through into the lounge where she found a notepad and pen in her mum's pile of magazines. She sat down and chewed the end of the pen a moment. Then she wrote her mum a long note. It was the first time she'd written anything at length for some time. It felt weird. Her writing was appalling, but she got it down. Told her mum she was going away for a while. Told her she was sorry, but she'd be back to look after her as soon as she could. She divided up the money and left five thousand on the table, more than enough to clear her mum's debts and pay the rent for a few months. She wrote she'd send more soon but implored them not to look for her. Then she signed her name and put a single 'X' at the bottom.

Alice didn't have a suitcase or even an overnight bag, but she didn't have much to pack anyway. She gathered up what she did have - jeans, hoodies, underwear - and stuffed it all into the same blue plastic sack they'd given her at Crest Hill. Then she took the rest of the money and quietly padded across the landing to Orla's flat. It was late, but Alice could hear the TV was on, some soap, by the sound of it. She knocked and waited, heard sounds and movement from the other side of the door. Then it opened.

"Oh, Alice dear. You all right?"

Alice smiled. "Can I come in?"

Orla looked puzzled but stepped aside. Alice went through into the front room and took out the money.

"I've got this money I want you to keep safe." She spoke fast, as though if she didn't get the words out, she'd lose her bottle. "Don't ask me where it came from, please. But I didn't steal it, I swear on my mum's life. It's for her. I've got a new job and I need to go away for a while. Can you keep an eye on her - and use this money for any care or medicine she needs?"

Orla stood in the doorway. Her expression was one of shock. But it was over-the-top - like she was on one of her crappy soap operas and wanted the audience to know she was confused.

"Where are you going?" she asked.

"I can't tell you. Sorry. Can you do this for me?"

Orla shuffled over and sat on the edge of her chair. "Of course I can. But I'm worried, Alice. You've only been home a second and now you're off again. I mean, I don't blame you. It's getting to be a real dump around here, but still - your ma."

Alice breathed heavily. "I know. But it's my only option. Here." She handed her the brown paper bag. "There's five thousand pounds in there. Spend it on whatever mum needs, whatever you need too. I trust you."

Orla accepted the money and held it in her lap without looking at it. "She is getting worse you know. I've noticed it lately. Terrible thing it is."

"Yes. I know. But doing what I'm doing, I can help her. Get her the best medicine. The best care." Alice paused. "Where is she tonight? Do you know?"

A look of dismay dampened Orla's usual demeanour. "I saw some man in a flash car outside earlier. Beeping his damn horn. She went with him. Sorry, Alice. She'd told me she'd packed that in too."

They both nodded in unison. Slowly. Deliberately.

Didn't look at each other.

"I have to go," Alice said. "Thank you, Orla. And whatever happens. Whatever you hear. I want you to know, I'm okay. I know that sounds weird and cryptic, but you have to trust me."

She gave Orla a brief hug and moved towards the door. "I hope you know what you're doing, Kid," Orla said as

Alice got to the front door to let herself out.

She stopped, her hand on the door handle. "Yeah, me too," she replied. Then she opened the door and was gone.

TWENTY-EIGHT

ALICE TOSSED AND TURNED ALL NIGHT. GOING FROM TOO hot, to too cold, and back again. She was too wired to sleep. Too full of questions. She also had one ear on the front door all night. Hoping her mum might return. But she didn't.

By morning she was still not home. Alice got up at six and showered, she even washed her hair - a rare occasion for her - but she didn't know when she'd get the chance again. Once washed, and her hair moussed and blow-dried, she made herself some breakfast. Toast. Left in too long. Burnt. Top layer scraped off in the sink. Plenty of butter. As she ate, she pulled the piece of paper from her back pocket and read the address. It was somewhere in Essex near Epping Forest. A few hours by tube. She looked at the clock on the mantelpiece, 7 a.m. Plenty of time.

She finished her toast and placed the dirty plate in the sink. She gave it a rinse and put it on the draining board. Then she gave the room a once over, picked up her sack of clothes, and left. There was no point hanging around.

She took a fifty from the money on the table and bought

herself a can of Coke and some more cigarettes at the station shop, and a tube ticket from the machine once she had some change. Shoving her hand in the machine to collect her ticket, she smiled at the irony. Paying for her journey for once, as she fled her old life towards one of crime and killing.

She took the tube to Mile End and then jumped on the Central line. It was rush hour. People were crammed up against each other. But Alice held her ground, with sharp elbows, as commuters bustled and shoved on all sides. Today her mood was high, and she felt invincible, almost to the point where she was willing someone – anyone – to invade her space, barge into her, give her something to react to. She'd have absolutely destroyed them. Nonetheless, as each station came and went, her tube carriage emptied out. By the time it reached Alice's destination - Theydon Bois - she was the only passenger left.

After exiting the train, she stood on the platform to gather her bearings. The clock hanging from the roof told her it was ten minutes to eleven. She was to take a left out the station and meet whoever was collecting her on the corner of Theydon Green.

She did as instructed, taking her time as she strolled through the pretty village. It felt absurd to be in such a quaint, picturesque setting. Though from what Alice already knew of Caesar, he probably got off on this juxtaposition - training her to be an elite killer in a place so serene.

The car was already waiting for her as she moved down Station Approach onto Poplar Row. Same car as yesterday, a large black BMW with blacked-out windows. As Alice neared a large man dressed in a perfect Alice in Wonderland costume climbed out of the driver's seat.

"There you are, my dear. You all set?"

Alice nodded, somewhat taken aback at the vision in front of her. Davros Ratpack was a big man with big hands, big chest, big legs. To see him dressed this way, complete with blonde wig and six-inch heels, was rather off-putting. But Alice liked it. He looked good. Fun, but scary, well over 7 feet in his heels. It didn't help the absurdity of the situation, but she had to accept it - life was going to be crazy from here on in.

"Can I put this in the boot?" Alice asked, holding up her sack.

"Sure thing. Here we go."

Davros moved around the car and popped open the boot. Inside were all the shopping bags, from her expedition with Caesar.

"He kept them all."

Davros looked her up and down. "Well, we can't have you walking around like some street urchin, can we? Not if you're going to be on the team." He moved his face close to hers, enunciating every syllable. "Elite Assassin Network. *Elite.*"

Alice stepped back. "I understand." Then, smiling, "Is that my training then? How to become part of the elite?"

Davros took the sack from her and placed it in the boot. "Oh yeah, next few months are going to be like Pygmalion." He slammed the boot shut. Alice frowned. "My Fair Lady? You know, about the professor who teaches some poor cockney lass to be all posh." He moved around and opened the back door for Alice. "Though in this version there'll be more guns."

Alice climbed in the back seat and was surprised to find a man, sitting in the passenger seat in front.

"This handsome devil is Spitfire Creosote," Davros sneered, in his nasally, Mancunian drawl. "Spit, meet Number Six."

Davros got in and started the engine as Spitfire Creosote turned and hit Alice with a textbook handsome-guy smile. All white teeth and twinkly eyes.

"Pleased to meet you, Number Six," he said. His voice was deep, and he was well-spoken. He took Alice's limp hand in his. "What amazing eyes you have."

"Thanks," was all Alice could get out.

To say Spitfire Creosote was handsome was an understatement. He had short, cropped hair brushed to one side, and the sort of crystal blue eyes you could get lost in forever. His skin was blemish-free and he had dimples in all the right places. Stubble too. And those lips. Just the right amount of fullness. So kissable, Alice might have thought. If she could think straight.

"I've heard a lot about you, Number Six," he purred. "It's going to be an interesting few weeks I'd say." His perma-smirk dropped a moment and he glanced at Davros. "You are eighteen, yes?"

Alice nodded. "Yes. A few months ago."

"Wonderful." He considered Alice, his eyes dancing up her legs, lingering on her chest. Then he winked and turned back in his seat.

Damnit.

He knew what she was thinking. Men like him always

knew. The annoying thing was he wasn't even her type. She liked grungy guys. Long hair. Tattoos. Or she had done, before Crest Hill. Being inside with all those girls had pulled her in another direction. She thought of Jacqueline and wondered what she was doing. Wondered if she ever thought of her.

"Here we are," Davros announced, breaking Alice's daydream.

She peered out the window as Davros pulled into the driveway of a large house and turned off the engine. It was a standard, two-story abode. Four bedrooms, at a guess. It was set in its own grounds on the outskirts of woodland. Maybe once it had been the groundskeeper's cottage. Alice read the sign on the wall, Honeysuckle House. There it was again, that mordant juxtaposition.

"This is where I'm going to be training?" Alice asked.

"Sure is," Davros replied. "You were expecting something else?"

Alice sniffed. "Yeah, I guess I was."

Davros laughed. "Me too, when I first came here. That's the point though, isn't it? No one would ever suspect it's a training ground for elite assassins. Clever is our boss."

"Is Caesar here?"

"No. You won't see him for a few weeks," Spitfire told her. He clicked off his seat belt and opened his door, before leaning back to face her. "Initially it's going to be me, you and Davros. Nice little threesome, don't you think?" He gave a wonky grin and got out, opened Alice's door. She slid across the back seat and Spitfire took her hand to help her out. He was wearing black suit trousers with a pale blue shirt, opened to reveal a tanned, muscular chest. Alice, still annoyed at herself, was unable to take her eyes off him. She watched as he took out a gold cigarette case and flipped it open before flicking a cigarette between his bulbous lips.

He saw Alice watching and offered the case. "Smoke?"

"Thanks." She reached for the case, scrabbling to remove a cigarette. She held it between her lips and Spitfire lit it with a gold lighter. They smoked together in silence for a few moments as Alice took in the scenery. With the tree cover, there was nothing else in sight but greenery. The air smelt good. She took a long drag on the cigarette and blew out a large plume of smoke.

"You look like you work out," Spitfire said, squinting out at the scenery. "I heard you were a Judo master as well."

"Not a master," Alice replied. "I was good though. I had to stop when I went inside."

"When you went inside?" He scoffed. "I thought you'd know about my past?"

He grinned. "Oh, I do. But I wouldn't call being in a borstal for girls, 'being inside.' It wasn't exactly Wormwood Scrubs, was it?"

"Piss off."

Spitfire pointed his cigarette at her, smiling. "There we are. The feisty spirit I've heard so much about."

Alice wrinkled up her nose. "What would you call it then, if not 'being inside'?"

"Living in a home for naughty girls?" He closed his eyes. "Paradise."

"All right you two," Davros snapped. "Come help me with this gear." Alice finished the cigarette and crushed the end underfoot. She joined Davros and Spitfire at the open boot and helped carry the bags of shopping into the house.

Honeysuckle House's small entrance hall opened out into a large open-plan ground floor. On the back wall there was a door leading through to a kitchen area and along the side wall a set of stairs up to the first floor. The rest of the space was taken up with mats, punch bags, and various pieces of scary-looking weaponry - knives, lances, nunchakus. Each of the windows was covered with a thick metal sheet so the only light came from two halogen strip lights on the ceiling. There was a high-definition decal image stuck to the front side of each window-covering, giving the impression of a normal front room if any ramblers or dog-walkers passed by.

"This is the main space we'll be using for fight-practice. That'll be with both me and Spitfire," Davros said. "Hand to hand stuff, knife-work - that sort of thing. You've already got your Judo training, so I don't see an issue. Now have you ever fired a gun?" Alice shook her head. Davros guided her through the space and into the kitchen which looked out on a large back garden. At the far end stood a long, concrete building. "That there's the firing range. You'll be in there a lot, I imagine. With Spitfire. Caesar will be here at end of the month for phase two."

"Phase two?"

"The fun phase. In my opinion. The psychological phase. Getting you in the right mindset to be a cold-blooded killer. You see the actual killing part – that's easy. You've proven yourself already. It won't be an issue. But living with yourself after your first, second, tenth kill - that's the hard part. But you'll get there. It does get easier, believe me."

"How many people have you killed?" Alice asked him. Davros gasped and put his hand to his chest in mock-horror. "Young lady, you do not ask an elite assassin how many people they have killed. Oh my god!'

Alice looked at her hands. "Sorry, I was only… I didn't think…'

Davros nudged her, laughing. "Calm down. It's only because you lose count after a while. Don't fret kid, you haven't insulted some sort of code or any of that shite." He leaned in close, his face less than an inch from Alice's. "Cheer up, Six. You've got to have a sense of humour in this game. Otherwise, it is going to get dark." He slapped her on the shoulder and walked back out into the main space. "Now let's get you settled in your room, and we'll send Spitfire out for some dinner. Do you like Chinese? Course you do. Come on."

Davros showed her upstairs while Spitfire brought the rest of the bags in from the car. The staircase was steep, and the steps creaked under Davros's large frame. At the top, the space opened out onto a narrow landing with two doors off to the left and three to the right. It smelt the same up here as downstairs. Of fresh paint.

Davros gave Alice the tour. There were three bedrooms, plus a bathroom and a separate toilet. Two of the bedrooms had bunk beds against each side wall and the third one contained a large double bed. Alice was to be in the first room on the left. She went in and sat on the bottom bunk bed on the right.

"Make yourself at home," Davros told her. "I'm next door. Spitfire is in the end room. I'm going to get changed into something less fabulous. Why don't you get settled and I'll see you downstairs in an hour?"

"What am I supposed to do?" Alice asked, looking around.

"I don't know. Relax. Spitfire will bring your stuff up in a tick. Try on your new gear," he swished the blond wig over his shoulder. "Remember, Six - the person you used to be is dead. Time to create a new persona for yourself." He narrowed his eyes and pouted at her. "Make it a good one. Make it fierce."

He breezed away, leaving Alice feeling smaller and more alone than she'd ever felt.

Apart from the two sets of bunk beds the room was sparse. Cold. It reminded her of the sort of army barracks you got in American movies. Full Metal Jacket sprung to mind. There was a small skylight over the far corner too high to reach. Alice walked over and stood underneath, squinted at the blue, cloudless sky. She felt uneasy. As though she'd exchanged one prison for another. She wished she could speak to her mum. Tell her she was sorry for leaving without saying goodbye.

"Where shall I put these, Madam?"

Alice spun around to see Spitfire in the doorway. He had three bags in each hand and one tucked under each arm.

"Oh. Anywhere is fine."

She watched as he walked over to the bed opposite hers and placed them down. The way he moved was so graceful. So controlled. His shirt was tight, and Alice could make out his muscular biceps under the material. He turned around and held her gaze. Neither of them spoke. Then he hit her again with that wonky, half-smile and walked out.

"Fuck."

Alice slumped onto her bunk and stared at the springs

on the bed above. So, this was to be her room for the next few months. After that, who knew where she'd be.

Alice had decided on the way here the only way she was getting through this was one day at a time. It was going to get dark and weird, and no doubt painful and difficult. But she could do this. She was strong. She was able. Whatever Caesar threw at her, she'd take it.

She closed her eyes and thought about what Davros had said. About taking on a new persona. It made sense. Alice Vandella had troubles, was confused, unpredictable. But Number Six? Whoever she became next? They could do this. Hell, they had to. There was no going back.

TWENTY-NINE

THE NEXT FEW WEEKS PASSED QUICKLY FOR ALICE. THERE were no clocks in Honeysuckle House, no TV either, so it was hard to know what time it was, let alone what day of the week. Soon the days merged into each other. The weeks just as much.

Davros woke her at dawn each morning and she was made to do a ten-mile run, all the way around Epping Forest and back with Davros coasting behind her in his car. The first week or so it almost killed her. It was dark, cold, wet. But after a while the wheezing stopped, the stitches ceased, and her stamina grew. She went from being miserable - and on the verge of tears the whole ten miles - to loving the challenge of bettering herself. As her timings went down, her energy grew. She even noticed the effects on her mental health. Felt sharper than she had done in years.

After her run each morning she'd shower, then eat a modest breakfast of porridge. The rest of the morning was spent on the mats. Sparring with Davros or Spitfire and, on occasion, both at once. The sessions were gruelling and unforgiving. Most nights she went to bed in pain. She had black eyes, a swollen lip, grazes - not to mention a nasty slash on her right shoulder from a wayward shuriken star that required a few stitches. Davros had obliged, telling her she'd stitch the next one up herself. It was all part of the training. A concise knowledge of first aid was a must for operatives in the field.

Despite all this, however, Alice found herself enjoying her training. Davros and Spitfire were hard taskmasters, but she could sense herself growing faster, stronger, more skilful. By the second week, she could easily disarm both men. At the start of the third, she knocked Spitfire out with a stunning elbow spin as he attempted a stranglehold. Praise wasn't given, and it was made clear any cute talk was reserved for after training. In the heat of the session, it was all about focus and discipline. Two things Alice had always struggled with in the past, especially when the bats were out. But with the added impetus of injury - or even death - if she put a foot wrong, she quickly learned to harness and utilise her raging, chaotic energy.

Shooting practice was her favourite part of each day. Mainly because she spent it alone with Spitfire. He'd often stand behind Alice and put his muscular arms around her. To help with her aim, he said. Alice seemed to have a lot of issues with her aim initially. But after only a few weeks she couldn't fake being a bad shot any longer.

Spitfire was impressed with her. Said he'd never seen shooting like it. Together they went through the whole range of firearms, from Berettas and Glocks to a particularly powerful Magnum Desert Eagle that sent Alice flying into the hay-bales along the back wall. She mastered the handgun quickly. After those came the fun stuff: Uzis, AK-47s, and Alice's submachine gun of choice, a Heckler & Koch HK416.

"Jesus, the poor bastard." Spitfire brought the latest target up the line and winced at the obliterated groin area. "You're not a man-hater are you, Number Six?"

Alice narrowed her eyes at him. "Depends on the man."

"Well remind me not to get on the wrong side of you."

Spitfire's attitude had altered over the weeks - from amused smirk to impressed smirk. Now he looked proud. He shoved a new target in the clip and fed it down the line. "Let's go again."

The nights were spent in her room. Caesar had sent Alice a stack of books for her to read - World history, geography, cultural customs, languages. Alice would never have chosen to read these sorts of books, but with nothing else to do she devoured them from cover to cover. There were obvious gaps in her education, and she enjoyed broadening her knowledge. She particularly enjoyed a book on etiquette and amused herself practising her stature and poise.

Then, one night about a month into her stay she was woken in the middle of the night with a loud commotion. She sat bolt upright in bed as Davros and Spitfire burst into her room wearing balaclavas.

"What the hell's going on?" she yelled as they threw a bag over her head and tied it tight around her neck. She felt hands on her wrists, forcing them behind her back. Tying them tightly with rope. She struggled as best she could but even with all she'd learned these last few weeks she was no match for Davros's bulk.

"Don't fret, kid. We're going on an adventure," Davros whispered, as he threw her over his shoulder and carried her downstairs.

"Where are we going?" Alice cried. "Tell me." She was only wearing a thin t-shirt and cycling shorts and the night air bit at her skin as the front door opened. She heard feet crunching on gravel, the beep of the car as it was opened remotely. "Please, let me go."

She was expecting to be bundled into the back seat, expecting the smell and feel of soft leather. So, when she felt the rough carpet of the car boot against her skin she began to panic.

"Piss off, what are you playing at?" she yelled, but Davros had already slammed the boot shut. Alice kicked around some more then went silent, listening. She heard the doors being opened and the suspension rocked to one side as Davros got in. Then Spitfire. Then the engine roared into life, and they set off.

"Help!" Alice yelled as loud as she could. If this was some kind of test, then the point was surely to escape. If it wasn't a test, then she definitely needed to.

"Keep it down," she heard Spitfire say. "We're going on a trip to the woods, that's all. Nothing to worry about."

"So why am I in the boot with a bag over my head?" Alice yelled back. But they'd already turned the car stereo up to drown her out. Some terrible 90s house track. As if it couldn't get any worse.

While the car sped on into the night, Alice planned her move, scrabbling around as best she could in the confined space, searching with her trussed-up hands for rough edges

- where she might be able to cut the rope free. But there

was nothing. The boot was empty. All she could do was lie there and wait.

They'd been travelling for over an hour when Alice felt the car begin to slow. With some effort now she managed to reposition herself, so she was on her back with her knees bent and her feet facing outwards. The idea was she'd kick out as soon as she heard the boot open, hopefully inflict some damage to one or both of them and buy herself some time. The car was coming to a stop. The music faded. She listened. No sounds were coming from outside the car.

Then she heard the lock click open, felt a whoosh of cold air on her bare skin.

"Go to hell." She kicked out with all her strength but found nothing to connect with. Her legs dropped heavily against the edge of the boot, eliciting laughter from both sides. Hands grabbed at her, pulled her out of the boot. Still holding onto her they led her away from the car. Alice could feel mud and grass beneath her feet.

They'd walked a few hundred yards before she felt a firm hand grip her shoulder.

"Far enough," Spitfire said. She sensed him leaning in. "Now go with this, Number Six, all right? The more you struggle, the more you yell, the worse it will be. Understand?"

Alice nodded in agreement as she was spun around. She felt something cold against her neck. A knife. Then her t-shirt was pulled tight and the knife ran down the length, cutting it open.

"Hey," she yelled as they ripped her top clean off. She was wearing a sports bra underneath but with her arms around her back and the cold air biting at her naked flesh, she felt exposed. Vulnerable. Maybe that was the idea.

The cycling shorts were next, the knife sheered them off in one fluid motion, so she was standing in only her bra and pants, freezing cold, bound, and with a bag on her head. To say she'd had better nights would be an understatement.

"Kneel," Davros told her.

Alice did so, terrified now, half expecting the cold metal of the knife to slice her throat open. Had she messed up somewhere? Was she to be executed and left here miles from anywhere? Away from her mum?

A million more thoughts whizzed through Alice's brain. The chatter of the bats was deafening, the pressure behind her eyes just as intense. Her skin was ice cold, but her insides raged with fury and heat.

She sensed one of the men move behind her. Felt the knife on her back. Was this it? She heard the car engine fire up. Felt the knife move down her body. Then it sliced through the ropes around her hands. A foot on her back pushed her forward but her hands were free. She managed to break her fall. She rolled onto her side and got herself upright. The rope around her neck was tight but with some effort, she managed to undo it. She removed the bag from her head and gasped a big lungful of the night air. Just in time to see the tail lights of the car fade into the distance.

THIRTY

"You total shitbags," Alice shouted after the car. "Come back, you bastards."

But it was no use. They weren't coming back.

She huddled into herself for warmth, her eyes darting left and right as they became accustomed to the darkness. From what she could make out, she was on the outskirts of a forest. Far from anywhere. Not a house or even a streetlight in sight. She stamped her feet on the soft earth, she knew she had to keep moving if she was going to survive.

Running some of the way, walking the rest, she set off in the direction of the car. It would have been heading for a road, so it made sense. But after that, she was on her own.

Her feet were like blocks of ice and her hair and soaked wet with mist when she reached a road. Though hardly a major thoroughfare. There were no streetlights along the stretch of pocked asphalt. No road signs either. A quick assessment and Alice took a left, following the road down a steep turn where it disappeared around a dense area of trees.

All she had was her instincts to guide her as she continued on. It was another few miles before she saw a strip of lights in the distance. They were red and uniform and went up into the sky. Some sort of TV antennae or aviation mast. Alice remembered seeing something along those lines on the drive to Honeysuckle House. She closed her eyes and pictured the scene in her mind's eye. The structure had been over to the left as they drove towards their destination, maybe a few miles from the house. If she trusted her memory, then the lights were facing the road. That meant, if it was the same mast, the house was on the far side of it.

Alice remembered too that the house was in a small dip, not a valley as such but not far off. If she headed in a diagonal line from where she was now, she should be able to see it soon enough. Would know she was heading in the right direction at least.

There were fields on all sides with high walls and sharp-limbed hedgerows blocking her path. But the quickest way was through. Alice pushed on, ignoring the bruises and cuts she received as she made her way towards the light. For the first hour or so of this torment – this trial of attrition - she'd wanted to cry, to scream at the unfairness of her plight. But now she fell into a zen-like calm. Acceptance was the key. She'd read that somewhere - or Jacqueline had said it - but now it made perfect sense. Every part of her was numb with cold, her hair was stuck to her face. But she wasn't giving in. This was a test, and she wasn't going to let any*thing*, or any*one* better her.

The lights were getting closer and there was now a faint glow below the horizon Alice hoped might be a house. Some kind of civilisation at least. With a renewed vigour she picked up her pace, running across the field. She'd gotten halfway across when her foot stepped into some sort of burrow. She screamed out as her foot got stuck there and her ankle twisted painfully under her. She fell forward, smacking her head against a large rock that stuck out of the earth.

Her vision spun; she saw stars but remained conscious. Just about. Surviving now on pure instinct. Life preservation. She was freezing, her body ached, and her head throbbed. A surge of emotion bubbled up into her stomach, but she pushed it down. She sat upright. Blood ran down her face from a cut on her forehead. But she was lucky. If it had knocked her out that might have been it. Alone, dressed only in her underwear - it wouldn't take long for hyperthermia to set in.

Alice got to her feet. Every muscle was tense. Partly with cold, partly with rage. Partly with determination too. She set off, limping but at speed, dragging her damaged ankle behind her. Full of endorphins and fury. Another half-hour and the distant glow showed itself to be an electric light. Another twenty minutes and it was clear - it was coming from a house. Another mile and she could see the familiar gables of Honeysuckle House. She'd done it.

The birds were tweeting in the trees and the sun was slowly rising over the hillside as she got to the driveway and shuffled up to the front door. She felt pathetic, broken, less than human. But she'd survived.

She pushed at the door. Locked. She raised her weary arm and banged hard on the wooden panel, using the heel of her fist. No answer. She banged again. A light went on. She heard movement on the other side. Then, slowly the door opened to reveal the immense figure that was Beowulf Caesar.

"Number Six," he growled. "What a treat to see you. Do come in."

He went back into the house and Alice followed, slamming the door behind her.

"W-w-where are-are those pricks?" she asked, with chattering teeth.

Caesar waved the question away. "Gone. For now. Come, warm yourself." He continued through into the main space which was now furnished with two large armchairs and a bearskin rug where the mats and pads once were.

Caesar picked a dressing gown off one of the chairs and threw it at Alice. She caught it one-handed and wrapped it around herself. It was warm and soft and felt good against her icy skin.

"I take it that was all part of my training?"

Caesar sat back in the nearest armchair and crossed his fingers over his stomach. "I've heard good things about your progress, Number Six. They say you're a natural. Very skilled."

Alice shivered. The embers of rage still surged through her system. The bat's screams were still incessant across her nervous system.

But as before, Caesar's words had a way of lifting her spirits. "I've enjoyed it," she told him, lifting her chin up. "Most of it, anyway."

Caesar gestured at the chair opposite. "Join me, please. Your ordeal is over."

Alice sat, as Caesar leaned forward, watching her intently. She adjusted herself on the seat and stared back at him, holding eye contact for long after it felt comfortable. Everything here was a test.

"Congratulations, Number Six," Caesar said. "You've completed the first part of your training. Passed with flying colours."

Alice ran her fingers through her dank hair and twisted it back into a loose bun. "So, what now?" she asked.

Caesar raised one eyebrow. "Now the fun begins. Well, I say fun, it's going to be a total horror show for you. But it'll be fun for me." He stood up and walked around the back of Alice's chair. "Get through this next month and your place in the organisation will be guaranteed. Now, I make it a few minutes after five. Go get a shower and meet me down here in half an hour."

Alice turned to face him. "But I haven't slept, I'm tired out, I'm bleeding…'

"That's right, my dear," Caesar snarled. "Did I say this was going to be easy at any point? Did you expect this to be a bloody holiday?"

Alice bowed her head. "No, but I thought…'

"You are training to be an elite assassin," Caesar told her. "Yes, you've proven yourself to be a fierce fighter, a good marksman-sorry-person, and tonight you've proven your mettle and determination. But now comes the real test. So, as I say - get a shower and meet me down here in half an hour. Because I promise you, Number Six, it's going to get a whole lot worse before we're finished with you."

THIRTY-ONE

WHATEVER ALICE HAD BEEN EXPECTING, THE NEXT MONTH'S training with Caesar was harder and more debilitating. She was subjected to a series of what you could only describe as torture sessions. Starting with a whole day and night standing facing the wall with her fingers high above her head, legs spread apart, and her feet pushed back. The forced angle meant she was up on her toes the whole time with most of her body weight supported on her fingers. It was a stress position, designed to break her mentally and physically. The fact Caesar was in her ear all the time, asking her if she wanted to quit, telling her there was a nice hot pizza and a cold glass of Coke waiting for her when she did, didn't help. But Alice kept her focus. Ignored the harpy's call. She'd read about psychological torture whilst in Crest Hill. The CIA, or whoever, would work on breaking people down - deconstructing their personality, so they could build them up again, gain their trust. It was weird, but knowing what Caesar was doing, why he was doing it, helped. Alice could step out of her predicament and observe what was going on as a passive onlooker. She even started to enjoy each challenge. Enjoyed the mental and physical workouts. Feeling herself growing stronger and more invincible by the day. Then there were the bats. That manic, creative energy, beating its wings across her soul. It was a valuable asset, she realised. When harnessed correctly. Her senses were heightened, her mind strong, impenetrable.

Two days standing against the wall and Caesar called time on the session. There was no praise of course. Though Alice was allowed to sleep for a few hours. Then she was taken, without food or water, to a concrete outhouse next to the shooting range.

"What do I do now?" Alice asked.

"You try and stay sane," Caesar told her, with a snigger. Then he closed the heavy door and locked it behind him.

Alice looked around the tiny concrete room. A single, naked light bulb hung from the ceiling, and in each corner above the door were two large speakers. Alice sat on the cold floor and closed her eyes. She knew what was coming.

Though she wasn't expecting the cacophonous Speed Metal music that burst from the sound system a few minutes later. The speakers buzzed with overload as the intense noise of the double-bass drum pedal beat against her bones and the singer screeched indecipherable lyrics into her soul.

Alice took a deep breath. She could handle this. She wasn't going to let the onslaught destroy her. She got up and danced around the cramped room. Pogoed up and down on the spot. She was weary. Delirious. She laughed feverishly at the insanity of her predicament. But she wasn't beaten. When Caesar turned off the music six hours later and opened the door, he found his new recruit sitting cross-legged on the floor, grinning demonically up at him.

"Got any Black Sabbath?" she asked.

Caesar stifled a smile, but he was impressed, she could tell. He shut the door. The music started again. The same Speed Metal trash as before.

Alice stood and carried on dancing.

Another six hours, or maybe longer, and the music stopped again. The door opened. Alice, exhausted now, remained standing. She swayed to the beat still pounding in her head.

"Well, well," Caesar said. "Ready for more?"

Alice winked at him. "You know, if you really wanted to break me you should have played Phil Collins." Then she collapsed, unconscious into his arms.

But break her he did over the next few days. More sensory overload. Followed by two days - or maybe three, it was hard to tell - of sensory deprivation. Alice was locked in a dark room with nothing else but her thoughts. Though clearly a small camera lens was positioned in the room somewhere - because whenever Alice looked like she might be falling asleep a shrill, high-pitched noise played.

For Alice, this was the toughest of all the tests so far. It was the darkness that got to her in the end. Staring out into an endless void she saw things. Shapes at first, then faces. People. Followed quickly by demons, devils, dragons. They spoke to her. Told her truths about herself. Told her she was already dead. Already part of their world. The demons swirled around Alice's head as salty tears poured from her eyes. She laughed, reaching out into the fractal black as a vortex opened up and invited her inside. A new world of evil. Home. The only place she'd ever exist. The only place she'd ever belong. And in that space, Alice fell asleep. Seven days of sleep deprivation and even the high-pitched squeal was a lullaby. It permeated her dreams and she met herself in the void. Met Alice Vandella. And there, with the demons sitting on her shoulders, Number Six put a knife through Alice's young heart and ripped her in two.

THIRTY-TWO

ALICE WOKE TWO DAYS LATER IN A SOFT DOUBLE BED surrounded by pillows. She sat up and looked around, recognising the room as the one at the far end of the landing in Honeysuckle House. She couldn't remember how she'd got here. Couldn't remember much, truth be told. She rubbed at her eyes and lifted the covers. She was completely naked, and she quickly checked herself for any injuries, any sign of interference. But she was fine. She felt good, lighter, like she'd shed an adverse part of herself.

She swung her legs out of bed, feeling the thick, shag-pile carpet between her toes. In front of her the large window had black velvet curtains pulled across it and in the corner of the room was a Regency-style armchair with a pile of clothes laying on the cushion. She padded over there and rifled through the clothes. A pair of black jeans, her size, from Dior; a black t-shirt, same make, plus new underwear, from Agent Provocateur, black with red trim. She lifted out the delicate lace knickers, inspecting them in the light coming in through a crack in the curtains. She'd never been into fancy underwear, but that was more down to how expensive it was rather than any real style choice. She slipped on the knickers and checked herself in the full-length mirror on the back of the door. She looked good. She'd lost weight since she'd been here. Which was understandable. But she'd toned up just as much. Her arms and legs looked strong. Her core too. She slipped on the bra, followed by the jeans and t-shirt. Everything fitted perfectly. Under the armchair, she found a shiny pair of black DMs and some socks. She sat on the floor and put them on. Then she went back to the mirror. Her hair needed a wash, but it looked okay. It was wavier than usual and her fringe looked long and thick. A thought crossed her mind, to ask her mum to cut it when she got home.

Shit.

The heavy realisation slammed into Alice's guts and winded her. She wasn't going home. Ever. Alice Vandella was dead. Metaphorically at least, for now. But, as Caesar had explained, once Alice joined the organisation, he'd have his people create a narrative for her death. A suicide perhaps. Car accident. It didn't matter. The point was, she'd be no more. No going back.

She thought of her poor mum. What she'd do when she found out. It'd kill her. Alice looked at herself in the mirror. She couldn't let that happen. If she had to defy her boss before she even started working for him, so be it. She'd get word to her mum somehow. Let her know she was safe and well. That she'd help her and look after her. She couldn't stand to have Louisa believe her only daughter was dead. Not after everything they'd been through together.

"Number Six?" It was Caesar, shouting up from downstairs. "Are you awake? I heard movement."

His voice was jovial, friendly. A far cry from the clipped monotone she'd come to know. The voice of her malignant torturer. Who'd flayed her mentally and physically this last month.

Alice opened the bedroom door and was welcomed by the smell of food. Her stomach rumbled instantaneously. She could hear movement downstairs, the chink of crockery. She went back into the bedroom a moment and over to the window. She opened the curtains. Outside it was a classic Spring morning. A bright sun ascending into a cloudless blue sky. The grass and leaves were moist with dew.

"Coming," Alice yelled. "One minute."

She walked over to the dresser opposite the bed and opened the top drawer. She was looking for a hair tie but all she found were pens and old notepads. The next drawer was the same, although she did happen upon a rubber band. That would do. She scraped her hair back and pulled the rubber band over a high ponytail. Then she checked herself once more in the mirror and went downstairs.

She was halfway down when she stopped. The downstairs room had been transformed once more. The chairs which replaced the mats and combat pads had gone, and in their place a grand dining table. Sitting on top, a vast array of delish breakfast items. Large silver platters of scrambled eggs, bacon, sausage, black pudding, along with bowls of fresh fruit, cereals, and a basket of tiny bread rolls topped with seeds and grains.

Caesar sat at the end of the table. On seeing Alice, he smiled and pulled out the seat to his right. "Good morning,

Number Six. I thought you were sleeping for England. How are you feeling?"

Alice paused. How was she feeling? Kind of empty. But not in a bad way. Lighter.

She continued down the stairs and sat down next to Caesar as Davros Ratpack appeared from the kitchen. Today he had on a bright-red wig, cut into a classic 60's bob. A French maid outfit finished the look, complete with seamed nylons and a tiny apron.

"Tea or coffee?" he asked, politely. "Umm, coffee. Please."

"Very good." He paraded back towards the kitchen.

Alice touched the knife and fork in front of her, spun the large white plate in a circle. She could see Caesar watching her out the corner of her eye. He smiled.

"Do help yourself." He reached over for a platter of scrambled eggs and offered it to Alice. "You must be bloody starving."

Alice nodded and accepted the eggs. Too right she was starving and normally she'd have had a witty comeback to this – 'What happens when you don't get fed for a week.' - but today it didn't feel right. She'd seen through the fabric of existence and being a wise ass didn't seem important presently. She piled a large spoonful of the creamy eggs onto her plate and followed up with two rashers of bacon and two sausages. Two bread rolls too. Caesar didn't take his eyes off her the whole time.

"You've done well, Number Six," he said. "Better than I'd hoped. You're a tough one. In every way. You're going to be a valuable member of Annihilation Pest Control."

Alice screwed her nose up. "Member of what?"

"Annihilation Pest Control. The cover for our operations. Clever. Don't you think? Seeing as that's what we'll be doing – annihilating pests."

Alice stuffed a whole rasher of bacon into her mouth and nodded. "So, does that mean I've passed my training?" she asked, between chews.

Caesar narrowed his eyes. "Almost. There's one more task for you to complete. But it's a big one."

Davros returned with a small cafeteria of coffee and poured some into a bone china cup by Alice's hand. "Milk?"

"Yes please," Alice said, but her throat was dry suddenly and the words all but inaudible.

Davros leaned over to the far side of the table and picked up a small milk jug. He placed it down next to Alice and patted her gently on the shoulder before going to back to the kitchen. Alice took a sip of the coffee. It was strong and red hot and it tasted amazing.

"So - a big one?" Alice said.

Caesar laughed. "That depends on how you look at it." He picked up a brown cardboard file from the seat next to him and slid it across to Alice. "It'll be your bread and butter soon enough."

Alice stared at the file. Didn't pick it up. "You mean…?"

"Yes. Your first mark. You won't normally get information in this manner of course. We don't like paper trails. Usually, it'll be coded messages. Posted to a secure online forum. I'll have our techie, Raaz Terabyte, give you a full briefing. Once you complete this final task." He picked up his cup and saucer and held his fat pinkie in the air, slurping down the last of his tea.

Alice chewed on some sausage, thinking. She knew this

moment was going to come of course. It was why she was here. But now, with the file in front of her, she felt a quiver of doubt.

"And I just – kill - whoever is in here?"

Caesar raised his eyebrows. "That's the long and short of it. There'll usually be a modus operandi for each job." Alice frowned and Caesar rolled his eyes. "The method to use - the theme of the kill, let's say. This one, I want it to look like a suicide. There's a suicide note in the file that you'll plant at the scene."

"A suicide?" Alice stared at the folder. "Will most of the work be like this?"

Caesar nodded. "Now you're getting it, Number Six. We aren't a group of cack-handed thugs who leave the mark in a pool of their own blood with a hole in their head. I mean, you might - if the specifics of the job required it – but most of the time a certain deftness will be needed. My operatives are artists, craftsmen. Most of the high-end jobs will involve eradicating pests without anyone being fingered for it. Forget unexplained homicides, Number Six. We are architects of suicide, freak accidents. It might not seem like it at first, but it's so much more fun. Much more stimulating than a wanton slash-fest."

Alice stroked the rough paper file. "When do you want this done?"

"That's my girl." Caesar looked at his watch. "I make it a little after ten. So, let's think- ten this evening?"

Alice baulked. "Today?"

"No time like the present." He nodded at the file. "Have a look."

Alice picked up the file and slowly opened it up. The

first page was a handwritten suicide note, and behind that piece of paper with an address written on it. A house, in Shepherds Bush. She placed both down on the table.

Then she saw the photo.

"What? No." Alice gazed at Caesar. Was this another of his sick jokes?

He was poker-faced. "It has to happen. She knows too much. You do this today and I've got all the proof I need you're the right person for the job. Do this, Number Six, and your life will never be the same again."

Alice tensed as she looked down at the black and white print in front of her. The photo was a few years old. The hair was shorter, the skin smoother. But the eyes looking back at her held the same balance of mischief and wisdom that had first intrigued Alice. She took a deep breath and closed the file.

"Fine," she said. "I'll do it."

THIRTY-THREE

Once fully briefed, Davros drove Alice back to London. She sat in the passenger seat next to him and gazed out the window. Looking at nothing. Lost in her thoughts. Ever since she'd opened the file and seen Jacqueline staring back, her head had been a muddle of perspectives and ideas. A strange numbness emptied her of emotion. The result of her training perhaps - or plain old self-preservation. She closed her eyes tight and rolled her head around her shoulders. Her back felt tight.

She turned to Davros. "What's with the get-up. You a drag queen?" It was an attempt to get out of her head, but she had been curious.

Davros side-eyed her, kept his eyes on the road. "Not professionally, but I've always enjoyed wearing a dress. I had been thinking about starting an act – Dolly Pardon – up in Manchester."

Alice laughed. "Dolly Pardon? You a fan?"

"She's all right I suppose. Good set of lungs, hey?" He sniffed. "I'd been toying with the idea. But never got it off

185

the ground. Then I bumped into Mr Caesar. I already knew him from way back. We went for a few drinks, and he told me about his new venture. Asked me to join. It was a no-brainer."

Alice considered this. "Where did you know Caesar from?"

Davros laughed. "Not a chance love. We don't talk about our past. You know that. That's all you're getting."

"Why Davros Ratpack?" was Alice's next question. "What's your real name?"

He sucked in his cheeks. "Come off it, Kiddo. You don't ask those sorts of questions. My real name is Davros Ratpack. I go by a few aliases, depending on the job, but that's who I am now. You do not ask an operative their original name – and you do not give yours. That sort of talk gets you eradicated. I'm serious."

A silence fell between them. Alice twisted a piece of hair around her finger.

"Weird, don't you think?" she said. "Words like 'eradicate', 'pest control' - why all the euphemisms?"

"To protect ourselves," Davros barked. "And the business. It keeps things civilised. You know Caesar well enough by now. He's old school. He's created an elite brand that our clients trust. We aren't thugs. We aren't mindless killers. We're artisans. Expert problem solvers. Think of your work that way, it's going to help."

"How many people have you – eradicated?"

Davros shook his head. "Jesus Christ, what's with all the questions? I don't think I've heard you speak this much the whole time I've known you?"

Alice tucked her hair behind her ears and slouched in the seat. "I don't know."

Davros side-eyed her again, smirking. "Listen, Kid. I get it. It's your first job. Not only that, but it's someone you know. It's fine to be nervous. But use that energy. Let it drive you, keep you on guard."

They didn't speak again until Davros pulled up on a side street a hundred metres or so from the address. "Here we are then. This is you. You got everything you need?"

Alice held up the small rucksack she'd brought with her. "Yes."

"Okay then." Davros leaned over and placed a large hand on Alice's shoulder. He guided her around, so she looked him in the eye. "Remember - this isn't about you. Or them. You are simply an instrument. A conduit, for someone else's wishes. You do your job and you do it well. That's where it starts and stops. Now, get out there and prove to us all you're as good as we think you are."

Alice held his gaze, then a look of steely determination fell across her face. "Thanks for the ride." She opened the car door and got out. She leaned back on the frame of the door. "Will you wait for me?"

"Sod that. I've got my own shit to do. Once you've completed the job, ring the number on the burner phone I gave you. It's the only saved number on there. You'll be told what to do next." He pointed at Alice, his face serious. "But if you fuck this up - can't do it for whatever reason - you're on your own. Understand? I'd suggest if that happens you make yourself scarce as quickly as possible."

"Why? What will happen?"

He leaned back in the driver's seat and gripped the

wheel, ready to drive away. "Make sure you get it done and no one has to worry about that. Now - off you fuck." He raised his eyebrows at her, meaning shut the door. Alice slammed it shut and the car sped off.

This was it. Her first job.

She checked her watch. Ten minutes after six. She had four hours. Easy. Though the timing aspect was never going to be the issue. She looked around. Got her bearings. Then set off towards Jacqueline's house.

THIRTY-FOUR

THE SUN WAS HOT AND BRIGHT AS ALICE APPROACHED THE large semi-detached house on St Stephen's Avenue. It was a nice street. A lovely house. Not the house Alice would have picked as Jacqueline's, truth be told - but she clearly made good money.

There were no lights on as Alice got up to the house. She walked straight past it, weighing up the situation as she did, eyeballing the doors, the windows. At the end of the street, she took a left cut down the alley, granting her access to Jacqueline's back garden.

The alley was deserted except for a black cat, curled up asleep on a green wheelie bin. Alice made her way down, counting the houses as she went. Jacqueline's back garden had a high wooden fence around it with a door in one corner. Alice reached over and felt for the latch. No padlock. She flicked it open and slipped through into the back garden.

Alice halted for a second, taking it all in. Jacqueline's house. She could see through the patio doors into the dining room and beyond that, the open plan lounge with its huge TV and cream couches. In fact, most of the décor was cream: the carpets, the footstool, the curtains, with the odd dashes of pink and light turquoise in the form of cushions and candles. Alice pressed her face against the glass, dismayed at how normal Jacqueline's house was. How tame it seemed. She wasn't expecting rubber walls, or chains hanging from the ceiling, but something with a little edge.

She slipped the rucksack from her back and rummaged around in the front pocket. She took out a small velvet pouch and opened it up to reveal a tension wrench and pick rakes. It was Alice's first time picking a real-life lock, but she'd done over a hundred test ones over the last few months. This one was rather stiff, but by now she had it down to a fine art. Was inside in under a minute. She stepped through into the dining room and closed the door behind her. Then she drew the curtains shut and went through into the main space.

Her instructions were clear. It was to happen upstairs. In the bedroom. Then, once done she was to set the scene. Create the narrative. This part required finesse and expertise, Caesar had told her. Why he wanted only the best in his organisation. He'd made the point once again as she'd left Honeysuckle House - the artistry didn't lie in killing people, but in making it appear there was no foul play involved at all.

Alice went upstairs and into the bedroom. Looked around. This was more like it. Red walls. Black bedspread. She removed a pair of black satin gloves from her rucksack and slipped them on before going through Jacqueline's drawers. Her heart raced as she pulled out bits of underwear, a suspender belt.

"You saucy minx." She held up a large purple vibrator. Anatomically correct, with bulbous veins running down the side. She switched it on and went cross-eyed as the tip twirled around.

The next stop was the wardrobe. A large, double-doored affair with the rail so full of clothes it was hard to see what was hanging inside. Alice pulled a few pieces out. Summer dresses, chunky knit jumpers. Again, it was a far cry from the sort of thing she'd expected to find in Jacqueline's wardrobe. In their sessions, she'd always worn predominantly black. To match her personality, she'd said on occasion. Was it all an act? Alice wondered. Done for her benefit?

There was a stereo on top of a large chest of drawers below the window with a stack of CDs alongside it. Alice walked over to inspect, lifting them up one by one. All the expected albums were here. Those they'd talked about. Bowie's Station to Station, Velvet Underground and Nico, Black Sabbath Vol.4. But every CD was brand new. Most had the cellophane cover on them. Alice flicked through some more as her heart sank and her rage grew. They were unopened. Had never been listened to.

She heard the front door open. Jacqueline arriving home. A surge of the old fight or flight shot through Alice's system, but she controlled it. She took a moment, slowed her heartbeat. Then, stealthily, she placed everything back in the drawers and moved over to the corner of the room, positioning herself so when the door opened, she'd be concealed. Once there she pulled a

Beretta pistol from out of the rucksack, and she waited. The days spent in solitary confinement - without food or water or knowing what time it was – had taught her how to wait. She understood now.

Downstairs Jacqueline was moving through into the kitchen area, directly beneath the bedroom. Alice heard running water; the click of a kettle being switched on. She gripped the handle of the pistol tight. Jacqueline was about to come upstairs and get changed before making a drink. It was only a hunch. But Alice was learning every day to trust her instincts. They hadn't let her down yet.

She closed her eyes. Remained still. Calm. Like a ninja, a shadow - she smiled to herself - like an elite assassin. It might take her some time to fully get to grips with her new persona, but she'd get there. And her instincts were correct. A few moments later she heard footsteps on the stairs. Heard Jacqueline's voice. She was singing. Some tuneless, wordless song. Alice lifted the gun. This was it.

She watched from behind the door as Jacqueline entered the bedroom and sat on the edge of the bed facing the window. She was wearing a white silk shirt and grey jeans, with black leather boots over the top. She crossed one leg over the other and unzipped her left boot, pulled it off. Did the same with the right one. Then she walked over and placed them down by the side of the chest of drawers. She had her back to Alice.

"Good evening, Jacqueline," Alice said, in her poshest voice. "It's so good to see you again."

Jacqueline froze. But didn't scream. Didn't turn even around as Alice stepped from behind the door and moved into the centre of the room.

"Alice?" She turned around, saw the gun. "What are you doing here?"

Alice gripped the handle of the Beretta tight. "I'd say it's pretty clear what I'm doing here."

"But…. I did what Caesar wanted. I don't understand."

Alice didn't blink. "I think you've found yourself to be what they call a loose end, I'm afraid. You know too much about me. About Caesar. It's nothing personal."

Jacqueline looked scared. "But Alice, I thought we were friends. I thought we were more than friends. Please, don't do this."

Alice snorted heavily down her nose. "I thought we were too. But now I see it was all a lie. You played me, didn't you?"

Jacqueline shook her head emphatically and stepped towards her. "No, Alice. That's not true. I felt something. You did too. I know it. Don't do this. We can sort something out."

She edged forward with her hands raised. Alice held her ground. "Was it all bullshit?"

"Excuse me?"

"Being into the same things as me. The music, books, clothes? What? All to gain my trust?"

Jacqueline's eyes were wide, pleading. "No. I swear it. There's a connection here. Fine, yes. I did some research on you. But only so I could relate to you better. But everything else was real. We both felt it." She was speaking softly now, a few inches away.

Alice's hand shook with tension, her finger quaking on the trigger.

"Shit."

She let the gun drop to the floor, as a lone tear fell from her eye. The gun landed on her foot and bounced onto the carpet. The tear ran down her cheek into her mouth.

"That's it," Jacqueline gasped, holding Alice's face in her hands. "You don't have to do this. We can run away. Me and you. We'll go somewhere no one can find us. Be together."

She reached up and wiped another tear from Alice's cheek. Then, slowly, softly she put her lips on Alice's.

Jacqueline smelt amazing. As always. Alice kissed her back, their tongues darting around in each other's mouths. It was sensuous, passionate. But also loving.

Alice reached with one to hold Jacqueline's face, sliding the other into the pocket of her jeans. They held each other for a moment.

The corners of the therapist's eyes crinkled as she smiled."I'm so sorry," she said.

Alice smiled back, before reaching up and jamming the paralyser ring into Jacqueline's neck. She held it there a few seconds, as Jacqueline bucked and shuddered and her eyes bulged with fright and shock. Then Acid stepped back and let the therapist drop to the floor.

"I'm sorry too," she whispered.

THIRTY-FIVE

"THERE YOU ARE, MY DEAR," CAESAR BELLOWED. OFFERING
Alice, a glass of sparkling Cristal. "Congratulations. You are
now a fully-fledged member of Annihilation Pest Control.
Feels bloody good, doesn't it?"

It was two days later, and Alice and her new boss were
sitting on the deck of a large riverboat on a quiet part of the
Thames. She took the glass from him and drank back some
of the ice-cold liquid.

"You know what, it does," she said. "This is the first time
in my life I've got purpose." She was going to add - 'Even if
it does mean killing people' - but she kept quiet. Didn't want
to push her luck. Caesar shared the same sardonic wit as
her, but he was unpredictable. Could turn just as quick.

"Cheers to you. By all accounts, you made a good show
of the therapist's demise."

Alice sat back and wrinkled her nose at the afternoon
sun. It was true. Her first job had gone better than she'd
even hoped it would. Once Jacqueline was incapacitated

with a sleeper hold, she'd stripped her naked and dragged her into the bathroom, hoisting her over the top of the bathtub and switching on the hot tap. Then it was just a matter of opening up her wrists with a razor blade and she was done. An obvious suicide.

After that, it was a matter of laying out props. Mainly the fake suicide note, telling of Jacqueline's guilt and sorrow after one of her patients - who she'd had a relationship with - had taken her own life. The name of that patient, Alice Vandella. Alice couldn't help but be impressed. The whole narrative was tied up perfectly.

She'd also managed to get word to her mum and Orla. Told them not to worry about her but stressed the importance of keeping their existence - and hers - a secret. It was safer that way. Caesar would never have to know.

Alice walked over to the side of the boat. It was a sunny day but not overly warm. She zipped up her new black leather bomber jacket. A souvenir from Jacqueline's wardrobe.

"What happens now?" she asked her new boss.

"One final bit of admin," Caesar said, standing beside her. "You have to pick your new name."

Alice thought a moment. "What is the deal with the names? I mean I get it - I think - but why so elaborate?"

Caesar gripped the railing. "I find it amusing, truth be told. But people find it helpful too. Think of it as an actor would. You're about to step into a new role. As a highly-skilled killing machine.' He closed his eyes and took a deep sniff of the salty air. 'You see, once upon a time I was a shy little queen with a name to match. Obviously, I won't tell you what it was, but you think anyone's going to quake in fear at the name Barry Clarkson, for instance? Brian Charles? No. Course not. So, you pick a strong name. One of power and distinction, which elicits fear in others. The only rule is - use your original initials. The only link to your past."

Alice looked out over the river. Watched as a duck swam past with two chicks in its wake. She thought again of her mum, of their life together. Broken. By illness and circumstance. Her mind drifted to a memory. Her as a young child, sitting on Louisa's lap.

"I've got one," she told him.

"Woah, there. Don't decide right away," Caesar said. "Give yourself time to come up with a good one."

Alice gazed up at him and grinned. "I don't need time."

"Oh? Do tell."

"Acid Vanilla," she announced.

"Acid Vanilla," Caesar rolled it around. "You know what, I like it." He raised his glass in the air and chinked it against hers. "Here's to working with you, Acid Vanilla. Something tells me it's going to be a real bloody riot."

THE END...

ACID VANILLA BOOK 2 IS OUT NOW!

. . .

SEVEN BULLETS

A woman driven by revenge. Seven deadly assassins. They will fall by her hand... one by one

Acid Vanilla was the deadliest assassin at Annihilation Pest Control. That was until she was tragically betrayed by her former colleagues. Now, fuelled by an insatiable desire for vengeance, Acid travels the globe to carry out her bloody retribution.

After all, a girl needs a hobby...

Leaving a trail of bodies in her wake, Acid journeys to Hanoi in pursuit of the next name on her kill list. Unfortunately, she has a couple of problems to deal with:

1. The shadowy organisation he's working for have the entire city gripped in fear.

2. He's the only man she's ever loved.

Getting to him means battling through an onslaught of underground villains. Not to mention her own muddled feelings. With time running out, a local man who needs her help, and the body count rising, Acid must use every deadly trick in her arsenal to survive. Can she infiltrate the organization and find her target before he finds her? Or will she pay for her hesitation with her life?

Fans of high-octane action and vigilant justice will be swept up in the nonstop thrill ride of Seven Bullets and Matthew Hattersley's Acid Vanilla Series.

CLICK HERE AND GET YOUR COPY NOW

ALSO BY MATTHEW HATTERSLEY

Have you read them all?

The Acid Vanilla series

The Watcher

Acid Vanilla is an elite assassin, struggling with her mental health. Spook Horowitz is a mild-mannered hacker who saw something she shouldn't. Acid needs a holiday. Spook needs Acid Vanilla to NOT be coming to kill her. But life rarely works out the way we want it to.

Making a Killer: Alice to Acid

How it all began. Discover Acid Vanilla's past, her meeting with Caesar, and how she became the deadliest female assassin in the world.

Stand-alone novels

Double Bad Things

All undertaker Mikey wants is a quiet life and to write his comics.

But then he's conned into hiding murders in closed-casket burials by a gang who are also trafficking young girls. Can a gentle giant whose only friends are a cosplay-obsessed teen and an imaginary alien really take down the gang and avoid arrest himself?

Double Bad Things is a dark and quirky crime thriller - for fans of Dexter and Six Feet Under.

Cookies

Will Miles find love again after the worst six months of his life? The fortune cookies say yes. But they also say commit arson and murder, so maybe it's time to stop believing in them? If only he could...

"If you life Fight Club, you'll love Cookies." - TL Dyer, Author

ABOUT THE AUTHOR

Over the last twenty years Matthew Hattersley has toured Europe in rock n roll bands, trained as a professional actor and founded a theatre and media company. He's also had a lot of dead end jobs...

Now he writes Neo-Noir Thrillers and Crime Fiction. He has also had his writing featured in The New York Observer & Huffington Post.

He lives with his wife and young daughter in Manchester, UK and doesn't feel that comfortable writing about himself in the third person.

COPYRIGHT